THE MARK OF THE
DRAGON
WHISPERER

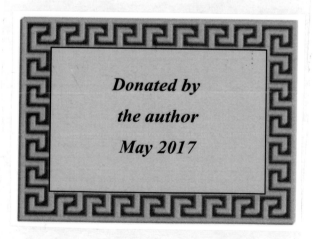

J.S. CASTILLO

C. 2

Published 2017 by CreateSpace

Cover illustration by RavenBorn Covers

Map by Jason Zucker

*Internal formatting by Lia Rees at
freeyourwords.com*

ISBN: 978-1-5307408-3-3

Dedication

To my talented and beautiful niece, Rebekkah: Never stop believing in magic...You see, magic is everywhere. All you need to do is close your eyes and open your imagination.

To my amazing husband, Vincent: thank you for always listening to my crazy ideas and schemes for my characters, and helping me not go completely insane with edit after edit! I love you!

To my sister, mother, and father: You've always told me to follow my dreams, and never judged me for my crazy imagination. This book I dedicate to you.

To my DAARlings: Thank you for letting me introduce you to my world of magic and sorcery, and for giving me so much motivation! I love and miss you all!

In Memory of Emma Elizabeth

Map by Jason Zucker

CONTENTS

PROLOGUE: SO SAY THE SORCERERS

KING JEDREK WAS ENRAGED. Combing his long, slender fingers through his hair, he paced the empty throne room; his footsteps reverberated against the dark gray walls as his black robes draped behind him, barely dragging along the polished black floor.

"No one tells me 'no'," King Jedrek seethed through gritted teeth. "Who do they think they are, denying a *KING* his request?!" In a rage, he grabbed his chalice and hurled it towards his servants. They quickly scattered out of the way as the elegant cup broke into a thousand pieces. The King was too furious to notice Sorceress Milla gazing at him through sad, gray eyes from the other side of the room.

"My poor King," the Sorceress thought to herself. He

1

had so much anger for such a young ruler. Not even thirty years of age, he was fit and tall; almost as tall as his father, who was twice his age when his soul left the mortal world. She watched King Jedrek pace back and forth until he looked up, his eyes locking onto hers.

"Milla," he whispered softly. His eyes showed relief, if only for a split second. The Sorceress blushed slightly. His features were breathtaking; his eyes reminded her of the greenest meadows in the spring, and his neatly trimmed beard covered his chin and jawline perfectly. Her eyes trailed up towards his ghost white hair and noticed how it contrasted with his dark beard, remembering the days when it wasn't always like that.

Milla moved quickly yet silently through the throne room, almost appearing to float on air; her long black hair flowed freely behind her as if in slow motion. The servants stared at her, gawking at her beauty. She had a slender build, flawless tan skin, and although she was tall for a woman, she still barely made it to the King's shoulders in height.

"They said no, my King?" Milla whispered softly, peering at him through her long eyelashes. She reached forward to touch his shoulder, only to have her hand swatted away like an annoying fly. She blinked in disbelief, then glared at the servants that witnessed the action, her eyes glowing a brilliant amethyst color. "Leave us," she snapped. Although she was beautiful to look at, the servants knew better than to go against the Sorceress' commands; the rumors of servants frequently vanishing from the palace was enough of a scare for them. Bowing quickly, they left without a second glance.

King Jedrek sat in his throne and huffed, almost in exhaustion, and began rubbing his chin with his first finger and thumb, grazing the stubble on his beard as he replayed the meeting in his mind.

***

The large golden doors opened for Jedrek. He entered the Hall of Sorcerers, his robes contrasting against the marble floor. The Hall of Sorcerers was quite spacious, or it might have been the multiple large windows that made it seem so. The light smell of lavender lingered in the air. Golden accents danced through the marble floor and columns, making everything sparkle when the sunlight entered the room. Fortunately for King Jedrek, the sun was setting, so the golden trimmings seemed to have a faint glow rather than their morning sparkle.

In the center of the room, surrounded by portraits

of Kings before—Jedrek recognized his father's portrait immediately—stood the High Sorcerers, each representing their Kingdoms. Each of the Kingdoms took over the four cardinal directions; Janulai in the West, Arana in the South, Baroody in the East, and Salzar in the North. A pageboy with rustic red hair that stood in the corner with rolled parchment in his hands began clearing his throat nervously as he read the scripture:

"King Jedrek, Ruler of the Eastern lands of Baroody, has made the request to the High Sorcerers—Kardos Starrain, High Sorcerer of Salzar; Tristan Belhearth, High Sorcerer of Arana; and Ezra Clearrune, High Sorcerer of Janulai—to be given the Gift of Dragon Whisperer."

King Jedrek felt his chest swell with pride as the pageboy stumbled over his words. *"Dragon Whisperer,"* he thought to himself. *"With that power, I will have control of the skies. No King in the history of mankind has ever made a request as bold as this...that is what made them weak; my father, my brother...everyone. They have no choice but to say yes. However,"* Jedrek hesitated in his mind, *"if they say no..."*

Jedrek observed the High Sorcerers. They all seemed so young to be considered so high and powerful; so young to have the responsibility of the

4

final say on this gift. All three were as tall as he was and were dressed in their formal robes: ivory silk with golden accents throughout each, as was the tradition when a meeting of great importance was being held.

"Your Majesty," the far left Sorcerer greeted as all three bowed in respect to the royalty in front of them. "Thank you for appearing today." He had blond hair, and his eyes were as the sea; a bluish-green color. Judging by his casual yet dazzling smile, King Jedrek knew this was Ezra.

"The pleasure is mine, Ezra. Tristan, Kardos," King Jedrek casually greeted the others. "Milla, the High Sorceress of Baroody, is not to be present?"

Ezra answered before the others could utter a response. "That is correct. She is no longer a High Sorceress for breaking sacred rules and responsibilities, in accordance with the High Sorcerer's Code," he smiled, without giving any other thought to the response.

The King nodded in understanding, but continued to glare at Ezra. *"I shall wipe that smirk off your face soon enough,"* he thought to himself.

Ezra smiled, as if he knew what the King was thinking, and turned nonchalantly towards the Sorcerer in the middle. "Kardos, would you like to begin?"

Kardos nodded silently. He looked the oldest of the

three, and that said a lot. He was also the tallest out of the three, and if the rumors were true, his enchanted sword wasn't far. He had light brown hair that was short and combed to the side, and piercing blue eyes that locked onto the King.

"King Jedrek," his voice resounded throughout the Great Hall, "as you know, the gift of bonding with a dragon is a rare gift to be had. Long ago, it was decreed that the High Sorcerers of each cardinal land would hold the ultimate responsibility: bestowing upon someone the Gift of the Dragon Whisperer. The subject would be nominated, and if chosen, they would receive a Mark. Customarily, Kings or other Sorcerers would nominate someone they believed to be worthy."

"You nominated yourself," Tristan, the third High Sorcerer, spoke bluntly. Jedrek studied the Sorcerer; he didn't *look* much like a Sorcerer. He had dark brown hair with what looked like eyes to match and, like the others, was fairly built, but not by much. His eyes, however, seemed to stare into his very soul.

"Only a person of pure heart and spirit," Kardos ignored Tristan's interruption, "would be granted the Gift."

There was silence. Jedrek arched an eyebrow and waited for the High Sorcerers to speak; to tell him that he was granted this gift and would soon bear the Mark.

"You have a dark heart, Your Highness," Tristan finally answered. Jedrek's eyes widened, and he gave the Sorcerers a scowl.

"Are you to tell me that *I* am not granted my request?" Jedrek inquired, his anger growing inside him. "Have any of *you* fought a war? Have *you* carried the burden of ruling a Kingdom?" Jedrek challenged, his own voice becoming louder than he anticipated.

"Well, *we* certainly didn't kill our *own* flesh and blood for the throne."

"Ezra," Kardos' voice was steadfast.

The King's face was neutral, but his eyes showed rage as his lips formed a thin line. "There's no evidence in the accusation claiming I killed my father...*or* my brother," he defended, his tone calm yet shaken.

"Care to explain the sudden color change of your hair?" Tristan commented, ignoring the warning glance from Kardos. "The true matter of concern are the whispers," he changed the subject. "Whispers throughout the Kingdoms of your — what's the word I'm looking for?" Tristan looked over at Ezra for advice.

Ezra shrugged his shoulders, showing a small smile. "Association?"

"Yes, that's the word. Your 'association' with the Shadow Realm."

Jedrek scoffed. "The Shadow Realm? *That's* your worry?" He let out a hearty laugh that echoed in the Hall.

Kardos raised an eyebrow, glancing uneasily to the High Sorcerers on either side of him, each mirroring his own expression. "So," he hesitated, "you are denying it?"

"On the contrary," the King confessed. "The whispers can be confirmed." The High Sorcerers fell silent. *"Not so talkative now, are you Ezra?"* the King thought to himself, enjoying the pleasure of catching the three men off guard. "The Shadow Realms are not dangerous. Well," he showed off a sly grin, his hands suddenly releasing small trails of purple and black smoke, "not to me. I have proved my strength to the *Varjo* and they know what I can do."

"You do not know what you are saying!" Kardos warned. "The Shadow Realms *are* dangerous; they curse your mind and possess your soul! You have no idea the power—"

"I know of ALL the power!" King Jedrek roared. Suddenly, the purple and black mass of smoke grew and surrounded the King, causing him to float. "The Shadow Realm opened my eyes...showed me the future...MY future! I was born to lead the Four Kingdoms, with dragons by my side and fire all around me. So you see, you have no choice! It has already been foretold."

"YOU KNOW NOTHING!" Ezra bellowed. In a rage, his hands began glowing a fiery yellow. "Jedrek of Baroody, you are as blind as Milla. Both your hearts are as dark as the Shadow Realm, and therefore you will NEVER be granted the gift; not you, not your sons, nor their sons!" Ezra announced. "So say the High Sorcerers. That is our final answer."

The dark, clouded mass surrounding the King began to fill the Hall. Kardos extended his hand to the left and a beautiful sword glowing a brilliant blue floated into his hand. He gripped the sword and stood defensively against the King. Tristan and Ezra's hands continued to glow with fire in preparation for a fight.

"Mark my words; you will pay for your insolence, along with all that are deemed 'Dragon Whisperer'!" King Jedrek bellowed. In an instant, the purple and black mass engulfed the King and he vanished.

**

"They underestimate me," King Jedrek fumed. He put his head in his hands in exhaustion, the tips of his white hair dangling enough for him to see.

"How do you plan on proving them wrong, my Lord?" Milla asked, kneeling beside her King.

Jedrek's mind was racing. He knew what he had to do; to prove everyone wrong—show them all he never takes 'no' for an answer. "We go to war," he finally replied. "If they will not grant me the Gift, I will take it by force!" The bitter King left his throne and walked over to a spacious window. The lands of Baroody were very vast, and very secure. He gazed down at one of the villages, catching a glimpse of the torches from his guards as they did their nightly patrol. "Anyone with the Mark of the Dragon Whisperer will be under my command." His mind began to race at the curiosity of what this Mark would indeed look like, realizing Kardos never indeed gave any specifics. *"I shall strip everyone of their clothes if I have to,"* he thought to himself. *"They will all be under my power."*

Milla stood behind the King, looking over his shoulder. "They will fear and respect you, my King." Jedrek turned slowly towards the Sorceress, brushing some of her hair behind her ear. She closed her eyes as her lips formed a small smile at the touch.

"They will respect *us*," he corrected. "Once I rule all four Kingdoms, you will take your place by my side as

Queen of Baroody—Queen of the Four Kingdoms."

She glanced away from his eyes and bit her bottom lip to hide a small smile. *"I will be his betrothed...not that royal brat of the North,"* she thought to herself, a twinge of jealousy rushing through her as she recalled the arranged marriage between the Kingdoms of Salzar and Baroody.

King Jedrek looked back outside. "They will not give me the Gift, 'so say the Sorcerers'," he echoed the rejection aloud. "Well, I will take it by force, and all will bow before me," Jedrek looked back at Milla, a wicked grin on his face, "so says the King."

CHAPTER ONE: THE GIFT

DON'T RAMBLE, FAYE." That was the advice given to Faye Haybear by her guardian, Marcus, moments before entering the chamber where their meeting with High Sorcerer Cato was taking place. Now, she was wandering around the red carpeted area, observing the pictures that filled most of the walls. She could see her reflection in one of the portraits; her green eyes staring back at the men in the pictures. *"One day,"* she thought to herself. *"One day that'll be me."*

"So Faye," The High Sorcerer called the young girl's attention once again. She turned toward the High Sorcerer, brushing some strands of her short, red hair behind her ears. Although his face was wrinkled from age, his hair and beard were a mixture of silver and gray, and his crystal blue eyes gazed at her through small round spectacles, his voice sounded young and smooth as honey for a man his age. "I hear you want to become a High Sorceress one day. Is this true?"

"Y-Yes sir, mister High Sorcerer, erm...sir," was all she could say without trying to ramble. She quickly glanced over at Marcus. He was fairly tall, with more hair on his face than on top his head, and a small pot-belly just barely showing. Although his face looked serious, she caught the faintest glimpse of a smirk peeking through his dark beard.

The old man chuckled as he smiled warmly. "Please, call me Cato." Even his smile was dazzling. "I've been around much too long to be called 'sir', especially from a sixteen year old," he chuckled again. Faye blushed and chuckled awkwardly as he mentioned her age. "Now," Cato cleared his throat, eyeing Marcus and Faye. "As you know, the time has now come for you to choose a trainer. This person will help you hone your talents in order to prepare you for your final test, which will take place on your twenty-fifth birthday. From what I understand, you wish to be trained under your guardian, Marcus. Now," he turned his attention toward the gentleman, "you have been caring for the child since she was...how old?"

"Seven years old, Cato." Marcus replied. "Her parents and I grew up together being great friends, and when they died—" he glanced over to Faye, trying not to show any emotion but was unsuccessful as he cleared his throat. "When they died, I watched over her; took care of her, taught her everything she knows about magic and how to defend herself."

Cato nodded in understanding. "That is all, Marcus," he stated simply. Faye raised an eyebrow and looked from Cato to Marcus. Instead of seeing Marcus' reassuring smile and caramel eyes, she saw the back of his head as he walked out of the Throne Room.

"Marcus?" she whispered, shocked to say anything too loud.

"Come along, Faye," Cato called. "Sit with me over here." With a tired groan, the old Sorcerer sat comfortably in one of the large regal appearing chairs, complete with plush cushions that were decorated with red and gold accents. Cato motioned for her to sit in the chair next to him. "Tell me about your parents."

Faye played with her green robe that Marcus made for her, feeling the fabric move between her fingers. It was a habit she picked up from Marcus, who would always grab random objects and fiddle with them when he was thinking or nervous about something. "What do you want to know?" she asked, shrugging her shoulders.

"Anything you remember," Cato replied.

Faye thought for a moment. "I remember my father's red hair," she finally recalled as she sat down next to Cato. "I remember playing with it when he carried me," she smiled at the memory. "My mother was beautiful. I remember my father saying how when the sun would come out after a rainstorm, it was so the heavens could gaze at her beauty."

Cato smiled. "And were they Sorcerers as well?"

Faye shook her head. "My mother explained to me how sometimes magic skips a generation or two. My great-great grandmother—my mother's side, not my father's side—had the gift. I don't remember if anyone on my father's side had the gift, but he didn't say much about it anyway." Faye twiddled her thumbs as she chuckled softly. "Sorry, I ramble a bit."

Cato shrugged, still smiling, but his face soon turned solemn. "If I may ask," he hesitated for a moment, "your parents—how did they...?"

Faye took a deep breath and sighed. "There was a fire," she said in almost a whisper. The memory flooded her mind all too quickly. "It—it wasn't like any fire I've ever seen. It was black...and purple...not even water would make it go away." Her voice began to waver, as she heard echoes of her parents' screams in her mind. Her arm felt hot as she recalled the burning sensation she felt all those years ago. "I tried to save them, but Marcus—he pulled me out. I've—I've tried to find spells...spells to stop enchanted fires. Marcus was the only one that seemed to stop it, but he—he doesn't remember." Her voice cracked, making her stop and clear her throat.

"Faye," Cato interrupted, holding her hands, "your magic has grown quickly over the years, and I completely agree that Marcus should be your trainer. A strong student should have a strong teacher," he complimented. Faye blushed at his words. She knew Marcus' talents were phenomenal. He would always have something new to teach her each day. "Now," Cato continued, "let us pretend that...that you *are* a High Sorceress, which is bound to happen if you continue your training," Cato nodded, his eyes twinkling with curiosity. "What would you do with that title?"

Faye thought for a moment, then shrugged her shoulders. "A title doesn't...really get you anywhere. It's what you do to *earn* the title that matters the most, right? I can't say I'd *be* the best, because no one is ever *born* the absolute best...we're born to *do* our best, and to do things that are *for* the best...for everyone."

Cato's sapphire blue eyes fixated onto Faye's green eyes. "What heart and wisdom for such a young girl. Faye, you are destined for great and wonderful things. I see it, and you will too someday." He paused for a moment, then blinked his eyes quickly and cleared his throat once more. "Now, off you go. Gather Marcus for me."

Faye hurried out of the room and into the corridor where Marcus was sitting. His caramel eyes lit up with pride as soon as he saw her. "Cato would like to see you," she said.

Marcus nodded in understanding. "Faye, wait here for me. This should only take a moment."

It was Faye's turn to nod. She sat down obediently as Marcus walked toward the door. He gave Faye one final, reassuring smile before pushing the door open and entering the Throne Room. As soon as the door shut, Faye leaped out of her seat and eagerly rushed to the door. She pressed her ear against the wooden door and tried to listen onto their conversation, remaining as quiet as possible. She could hear their muffled talking.

"—such a good heart, like her mother. Not to mention her gift of rambling..." Faye recognized Marcus' voice instantly and rolled her eyes.

"Which is why I am granting your request," Cato remarked.

"Because of her rambling?"

"No," she heard Cato sigh, "because of her good heart. I've been a High Sorcerer for many long years now, and I know greatness when I see it." There was a pause. Faye pressed her ear harder against the wooden door. Suddenly, the door swung open and the young Sorceress tumbled face first into the room. Faye's cheeks grew as red as the colored carpet she landed on. "I also know," Cato sighed again, his hand glowing a slight blue, "when there are curious eavesdroppers."

Faye looked up sheepishly at Marcus. He gave her a stern look, but she could see the tiniest smile creep across his face. "May I ask what the request was?" Faye asked curiously. Marcus looked over to Cato who only nodded.

"Faye," Marcus cleared his throat, "do you remember us talking about Dragon Whisperers?"

The young girl nodded. "It's someone that is selected by the High Sorcerers, and they are given a..." she paused and raised an eyebrow towards the High Sorcerer. His eyes twinkled through his spectacles. "Wait," she shook her head. "Are you...am I...did he...?" Faye couldn't find the words to say.

"Your heart is pure, Faye," Cato complimented. "You might be the youngest Sorceress to be given the gift of Dragon Whisperer. Use this gift only for the good of others; never use it for vengeance or hate. Do you understand?"

Faye nodded, smiling a small smile. "I understand." There was silence. There was no magic dust, nor mystic glow around the young girl. She looked around in confusion. "So...what happens now? Am I..."

The old High Sorcerer let out a small chuckle. "You will bear your Mark once you meet your dragon. This dragon will be bonded to you by your very soul. You will feel each other's emotions; their pain will be yours as well as their happiness, sadness, etcetera, and vice versa. Don't be surprised if you don't see or feel anything for the next few years; your dragon will find you when it is time, I promise." He walked over to the young girl and placed his hand on top of her head, mumbling a few words in a language Faye didn't understand. As if instantly, she felt her eyelids grow heavier until she couldn't keep them up anymore.

***

"*Faye...*"

Faye opened her eyes, letting out a small gasp as she sat straight up. "Hello? Is—is someone there?" she called out, but saw no one as she looked around. The forest,

19

being very peaceful, was a place Faye traveled to often in order to clear her mind, as well as obtain certain ingredients for her healing potions.

She stretched out once again on her bed of grass, admiring the softness of the ground and traced her fingertips on the rough base of the Grandfather Tree that provided her shelter from the afternoon sun. She called it the Grandfather Tree, because not only of its great height, but because it had been there ever since she was a little girl. She closed her eyes again and sighed contently, enjoying the peace and quiet.

"Bad dream, Sorceress?" a voice questioned. Faye knew the voice very well and smiled. The young girl opened her eyes to see her good friend Zachariah gazing down at her. Even kneeling beside her, he was much taller. His hazel eyes looked into her green eyes, concern written all over his brow, and yet she imagined him smiling under his cloth. Being part of the Elven Clan, all warriors had a silk cloth covering the lower half of their face, but with his grand height and long blond hair covering his Elvish ears, he stood out either way. Strapped around his right shoulder was his quiver, the normal home for his bow and arrows. She noticed he was in his usual hunting apparel; his pants, shirt, and cloak blending in perfectly with the forest, like Faye.

He was the one that taught her how to navigate through the thick forest of Janulai, and she was very grateful for it.

Faye sat up and stretched her arms. "No, Huntsman," she smirked as she called him by his title, "just a memory." She looked behind her and gathered her leather satchel that acted as her pillow just moments ago.

Zachariah raised an eyebrow. "I see." She could hear the hint of concern in his voice; he was always looking out for Faye, as if he were more a protector rather than dear friend. She played with the blades of grass and glanced away, her eyes staring at the fresh clovers underneath the giant Grandfather Tree.

"Clovers," she muttered. "I need clovers. Oh, and fresh dew—I'm getting short on that," she changed the conversation quickly. As she gathered clovers, Zachariah gently grabbed her hands and held them with his own. Faye looked at him through her red bangs that always fell in front of her face. He softly brushed her hair out of the way and then lifted her chin up with his index finger and thumb. She admired the irony of the soft, feathery touch his calloused fingers had.

"Faye," he whispered, "are you sure everything is alright?" Zachariah's voice was reassuring, though his eyes showed concern.

She hesitated, but finally answered. "I'm just nervous about tomorrow. I don't even know why *I'm* the one nervous, I'm not even meeting the High Sorcerers; Marcus is," she admitted, playing with one of the clovers she plucked from the grassy bed. "It's been..." she paused as she thought back on the memory. "Wow, eight years! Eight years since I stepped into that place."

Zachariah nodded as he stood from the ground. "I'm sure it's nothing to worry about. But then again, what do I know about magic and sorcery?" He shrugged casually, extending his hand out to Faye. Nodding silently, she accepted the help. She knew he didn't approve of magic. Although the Elven Clan had its history of using magic, he never believed it was right. While Marcus taught her the ways of magic and sorcery, Zachariah taught her the ways of survival without magic; how to hunt, track, and to stay hidden in plain sight.

Although the woods were thick with trees, rays of sunlight still broke through the canopy of leaves. Faye loved the forest. Whenever she wanted to clear her mind, she would always find herself in this place of serenity. "Zachariah, we've been friends for a long time, yes?" she asked.

The huntsman blinked a few times, and she imagined him smiling behind his silk cover. "Yes, Sorceress;

since the day you found yourself lost in the forest you now know well," he replied.

"I still don't think it ever rained as hard as that day," she whispered softly. "My powers were useless, since I can't—"

"Use magic when water touches your skin," he finished her sentence. "You were hopelessly lost."

Faye nodded. She remembered the night very well; the cold rain, the strong winds... "If you hadn't been nearby to save me..."

The huntsman softly shushed his friend. "No need for those kind of words," he assured her. "Everyone has those moments. But Faye," he raised an eyebrow, "why are you bringing all this up?"

Faye played with the edge of her satchel, feeling the smooth leather against her fingertips. "You get to travel everywhere." Zachariah let out a laugh. She had a feeling he already knew this conversation was going to be brought up, as it always was, and playfully pushed him. "Will you take me with you one day? I want to explore more than just these forests!"

"Don't worry, Sorceress," he said after enjoying a good laugh. "I'm sure once you receive your Mark, your dragon will—"

The forest became eerily quiet. Faye looked up at

her friend, horror written on her face. "Not so loud!" she hissed. She looked around nervously, making sure no eyes or ears were witnessing their conversation. "If one of Jedrek's spies were to hear you—"

"They wouldn't live to make it back to him, Sorceress," he assured her, searching the higher tree branches, already armed with his bow and arrow. Stories of Dragon Whisperers disappearing had been circling the villages since King Jedrek declared war on the surrounding Kingdoms two years ago. "I'm sorry, Faye. I shouldn't have—"

"It's alright," the young girl sighed. She could never stay upset at her friend. "I think we're safe. Let's keep going."

"*Faye...*"

The young girl whirled around and gasped quietly, her eyes scanning the forest for the source of the voice. There was nothing but trees and foliage in sight.

"Faye? What is it?" Zachariah stood protectively in front of Faye, still armed. The young girl didn't reply right away. She kept looking around, hoping it wasn't one of Jedrek's spies that now knew her name.

"You—you didn't hear someone call my name?" she asked finally. Zachariah slowly turned back towards his friend, raising an eyebrow.

"I heard nothing. Maybe it's your nerves getting to you." Zachariah took one last look around, and then put his weapon back in his quiver. "Come, I will walk you home."

Reluctantly, Faye followed. She assumed Zachariah was right, and perhaps it was her mind playing tricks. As she turned around once more towards the forest, her heart skipped a beat when she saw something moving.

Something *big*.

***

That night, Faye woke with a start. Someone had entered their hut and screamed for Marcus' name. She closed her eyes, pretending to be asleep as she heard someone walk near her bed. She could feel Marcus' hands fix her blanket, sighing softly.

"You're lucky she sleeps deeply, Brayden," he hissed as he walked away. Faye counted to ten, then quietly snuck out of her room and to the source of the two men talking, which was the small common area in their hut. She mentally reminded herself to thank Zachariah for teaching her how to be silent with each step and how to slow her breathing in order to keep hidden. Their home was larger than most of the homes in their village, but not by much. They had three bedrooms instead of two, and what Faye deemed the common area was slightly larger, which helped when multiple townsfolk visited in need of medicine.

"Marcus! You have to help me," Brayden Almastutter, the baker of the town, pleaded. Faye peeked around the corner. She could always spot him in a crowd; his corn-yellow hair was always a mess, and he was tall; taller than Marcus, even. She pictured Brayden standing next to Zachariah, and thought how it would be too close to tell which man was the tallest. "I don't know what to do," his cry brought Faye back to the situation at hand.

"Tell me, old friend," Marcus ushered him calmly, bringing two mugs to the small table. "Tell me what is wrong."

Brayden hesitated speaking, then took a large gulp of his drink as if for courage. "I—I have it," he uttered. Faye didn't know what 'it' was, but 'it' was enough to make Marcus' face lose color.

"Are you certain? Do not lie about something like—"

Brayden slammed his fists onto the table, turned to face Marcus, which unfortunately meant Faye only had a view of Brayden's back, and rolled up his left sleeve until it passed his elbow. "Does *this* look like a lie?!"

There was silence. Faye looked at Marcus' face, and knew whatever the baker had was very serious.

"The Mark," he gasped. Faye's eyes widened as she tried getting a glimpse of the Mark. What did it look like? Was there writing? Was there blood? Brayden rolled his sleeve back down as he sat in his chair once more, causing Faye to grumble softly. "Who...?"

"Maester Balsher; I was his apprentice before he gave me the shop," Brayden explained. "At first, I thought it was wonderful. I was truly...honored," he chuckled dryly as if he told a joke, "at High Sorcerer Cato giving me this news. My wife was so happy...now," he shook his head, "we have been praying the blasted Mark never appeared, my dragon never to show... please," Brayden stifled back a sob. "I have a good family...a wife and children...why now? Can't you, I don't know, cast a spell?? Make this Mark...this dragon...go away?"

"You know I can't UnMark you...it doesn't work like that," Marcus responded sadly.

"It needs to!" the baker cried. "You know what I've heard about Dragon Whisperers?! They get kidnapped...killed, even! I'll never see my children again."

"This..." Marcus tried finding the words, but sighed.

"I can't help you." Marcus lowered his head in defeat as Brayden cried loudly. Faye's heart ached for the man. His youngest child had just turned three, and if what Brayden was saying was indeed true...

Not wanting to get caught, Faye tiptoed back into her room. As she climbed into bed, she could still hear Brayden continue to cry. "I wish I was never nominated! This isn't a gift...it's a curse! A CURSE!"

CHAPTER TWO: THE MARK THAT WASN'T

I HAVE TO SAY, I'M IMPRESSED." Faye raised an eyebrow at Marcus' remark as she caught her breath. "Impressed? That's all you have to say?" she challenged. "We have been fighting all day, and all you can say is... you're 'impressed'?! I beat you! Fairly, I might add!" she huffed.

"Your weapons in a bottle might be handy now," Marcus nodded, pointing to the broken shards of glass on the ground and green goop stuck on his feet, "but you need to curb your emotions, and focus more. You seem distracted. That's how I've been able to strike."

"Only twice!"

"It only takes *one* mistake to end a life," he snapped. Faye froze at that statement. She had never seen Marcus so upset during her training. Slowly, she grabbed another vial filled with pink powder and poured the contents on his feet. In an instant, the green goop disappeared and he was able to move once again. He looked at Faye, his eyes suddenly softening. "Faye, I just...I want you to be able to protect yourself, but you can't do that if your mind is preoccupied. Tell me what's wrong."

Faye bit her bottom lip as she fiddled with the empty vial. "I'm just... confused." Faye looked up at Marcus. "Why did you pick me? I'm not good enough to be a...well, you know," Faye sighed, not wanting to risk anyone overhearing. She sat silently against a tree that still had a burn mark from one of the energy balls Faye attempted to strike at Marcus. She glanced down, fighting the urge to cry and fiddled with her thumbs until she saw Marcus' staff in front of her. Glancing up, she watched as Marcus placed his hand against the injured bark, causing it to glow a soft purple. Once he removed his hand, the mark was gone. It was as if nothing ever happened to the poor tree.

"Faye," he sighed, "You know what I see in your eyes when I look at you?" The young girl shook her head silently, tears in her eyes. He knelt down beside her. "I see hope. I see a better future than anything I could ever do. You have the power to change lives, Faye.

left the village. He ran away. You have to understand," he grabbed her hand, "with so many Whisperers disappearing left and right—"

"Well! Lookie 'ere!" a slurred voice interrupted, banging against Faye's chair. "Hello, purrdy lady!" the blond man grinned, his face and eyes flushed from the amount of alcohol he consumed. "Whuu-hic! What's in the bag?" he asked, lazily motioning towards her satchel.

Faye cleared her throat. "Nothing of your concern sir," she stated calmly, giving Zachariah a warning glare. She could see the fire in his eyes as the man continued standing too close for comfort.

"Awe, c'me on!" the blond man cooed, his breath reeking of alcohol. His shaky hands tried grabbing the satchel still around Faye's shoulder. "Lemme see!"

"The lady said no, you drunken menace!" Zachariah seethed. "Return to your corner and wallow in your beverages instead of wearing them," he motioned to the drunkard's shirt that was stained with alcohol.

"'Oy, masked -hic!- man," the man slurred, "Keep to yerself." He tried to grab hold of the satchel once more, this time pulling harder.

"Let me go!" Faye commanded, pushing the man away with an energy force that sent him flying into an empty chair. The tavern became silent. All eyes were staring at Faye and her glowing hand. She gazed down at them and saw a faint purple glow as her hands returned to normal.

"Did you see that?"

"She used magic…"

"Serves the man right, but…"

"What's this on your arm?!" a voice shouted. Faye felt her right arm being pulled forcefully and realized the second drunkard had grabbed her arm and raised her sleeve up. Gasps were heard throughout the tavern as onlookers caught a glimpse of scars covering her arm.

"She has the Mark!" someone cried. Faye looked around, shaking her head.

"No!" she cried out to deaf ears. "No, it's just—"

"Jedrek will be coming for her soon!"

"He'll wreck the village!"

"Call the Guards!"

"Make sure she doesn't escape!"

It all happened too fast. Faye pushed the tall man still holding onto her with another force field, trying desperately to run out of the tavern. Another man, more sober than the other two, grabbed onto her waist tight.

"Going somewhere, Dragon Whisperer?!" he growled through crooked teeth. She glanced in Zachariah's direction. In that short amount of time she watched as he had already leaped over the table, climbed onto the tall man and twisted his legs around the man's neck, causing him to fall down. Another man tried attacking Zachariah with a chair. The huntsman rolled off the ground, did a flip in the air and as he landed on the chair, punched the man, who fell with a loud *THUD*.

"Faye, run!" her friend cried. She didn't hesitate. Faye also didn't see someone was standing nearby as she collided into him and fell to the ground. The man was dressed in dark pants and a white shirt that showed off his physique. He stood tall, his brown eyes scanning the area, then towards the fallen girl. Faye stared back, a blank expression on her face.

"What's going on here?" he barked.

"It's her!" a woman cried. "She—she has the Mark!"

The man gazed down at Faye, a curious look in his eyes.

"LIES!" Zachariah cried. "Sir, I can assure you that—"

"It's alright, Elf." he stated nonchalantly. The crowd soon averted their judging eyes from Faye to Zachariah. "Where is this so called, 'Mark'?" he called out. The group of accusers were suddenly silent.

"Her arm!" one of the drunkards called out. "Look at it! It's covered in the Mark!"

"Really?" the stranger raised an eyebrow, his eyes giving a challenging look to the accuser. He then looked back down at Faye, his eyes once again lit with curiosity. "Does anyone here even *know* what the Mark looks like?" he asked, never looking away from Faye. An awkward silence filled the room. "That's what I thought," he sighed, extending a hand to help Faye up. Faye hesitated, but then accepted the man's help. Once she was up, the man lifted up her sleeve and observed the markings. He sighed in annoyance as he looked at the drunk. "I hope you aren't as stupid when *not* taking a drink, sir. This," he motioned to the scarring, "is not the Mark. Obviously, this is a burn from a fire. Am I right?" he looked at Faye once more.

She averted his gaze, embarrassed and suddenly ashamed. She felt him slowly loosen his hold on her arm as she covered her scars once more. Turning silently to the table she and Zachariah occupied, she placed a few coins on the table and walked away, not looking back.

"*Seems to me that everyone is so scared, they'll call anything the Mark,*" she thought to herself, fighting the tears in her eyes.

"Those imbeciles," Zachariah seethed. "I should've done more. I'm—"

"What happened, happened," she interrupted his apologies. "I'm just glad it's over."

"Wait!" a voice called out. Faye turned around and saw the man that helped her just moments ago. He grabbed her hand and dumped coins into it. "You shouldn't have to pay for that kind of meal, the entertainment was just horrible," he stated, chuckling dryly at his poor joke.

Faye smiled. "Thank you, erm...?"

"Oh, where are my manners? Tristan Belhearth. I'm—"

"Faye!" Marcus' voice cried out. Through the crowded marketplace emerged Marcus, relief showing in his face. "I thought I told you not to wander off."

"She was with me, Marcus. I made sure no harm came to her." Zachariah insisted.

Marcus studied the huntsman, and then slowly nodded his head. "Are you ready to go?"

"Yes, I just want to thank—" she looked behind her to find Tristan gone. "Wait, what—"

"Faye," Marcus sounded more insistent, "Let's go. I need to get ready."

CHAPTER THREE: THE OBTUSE STRANGER

FAYE WAITED OUTSIDE THE GOLDEN DOORS FOR MARCUS. She had no idea what he needed to discuss with the High Sorcerers, but it must have been important since he was dressed so nice. Casual garments were concealed underneath his complete Sorcerer apparel: an elegant dark blue robe with silver trimmings, his best shoes, and his wooden staff in hand that was decorated with four glimmering diamonds.

"When you meet the High Sorcerers, you always have to look your best," his words from earlier that day echoed in her mind. Faye was wearing her dark green hooded robe Marcus made for her, and just underneath

muttered, examining the portrait in his hands, "definitely filthy." He blew a thin layer of dust off the gold frame, causing Faye to sneeze.

"I think the High Sorcerers might," Faye quipped, rubbing her index finger against the tip of her small nose. "Or are you just too obtuse to realize that?" Faye challenged as she crossed her arms in impatience. She couldn't believe the audacity of Tristan but she was determined to set him straight.

The man stepped off the chair and raised an eyebrow in her direction, a look of surprise showing on his face. "Did...did you just call me...*obtuse?*" Tristan clicked his tongue in a disapproving manner, his hands tracing the edges of the picture frame he was still carrying. "Young lady," he warned softly, "You have no idea who I am. You have no idea what I am capable of in this world, so try talking to me a little more nicely."

"I don't care if you saved me from those drunkards or not! You have no right sitting in the High Sorcerer's chair," she defended, now annoyed at the condescending tone in his voice.

The man hesitated before speaking, turning towards the chair he was recently standing on. "Wha—the chair? That is—"

"Not yours! Only High Sorcerers can sit there!

Everyone knows that," Faye rolled her eyes, quite annoyed with the man. "I'm done talking to you," she huffed, walking past him and heading for the door.

"How do you know?" he finally asked, making Faye stop in her tracks.

"Know what?"

"How do *you* know," Tristan pointed a finger at her, "that I'm *not* a High Sorcerer?" he challenged. "You don't even know me!"

"Well, look at you!" Faye snapped. "The first obvious reason: High Sorcerers are old, have long beards, and wear their ceremonial robes all the time," she ignored Tristan's laughter as she stepped right in front of him. "Second, they're also kind and peaceful...they certainly don't stand on furniture and grab things that don't belong to them!" She snatched the frame from his hands and looked back at the empty spot on the wall. It was at that moment when she realized she had once again reacted before thinking. The vacant spot was about seven feet up the wall, and since she knew no levitation spells, there was no way she could reach that without climbing onto something. Groaning in frustration, Faye removed her satchel and dropped it on the floor.

"Well, this is just great," the young girl mumbled as she began to climb on one of the High Sorcerer's chairs.

Faye suddenly heard the man laugh even louder than before, and out of the corner of her eye she saw Tristan appear next to the chair with a large grin on his face.

"Well, well!" the man teased, leaning against the wall. "Looks like you're no High Sorceress, either. Climbing on chairs that aren't yours!" he mockingly scolded the young girl. "I guess we're in the same predicament. Young, disobedient..."

"Shut it," she ordered. "I'm trying to concentrate. I don't need you to distract me with your—" she stopped talking when the chair wobbled a little beneath her feet.

"Careful, girl. I would hate to see that pretty head of yours hit the floor from six feet high," he advised, his voice suddenly carrying a tone of caution. "Or is it *you* that is too obtuse now?"

Faye rolled her eyes in annoyance. "I've climbed trees much taller than this. I think I'll be—"

"FAYE!" a voice roared in the room. In a panic, Faye jerked her head towards the sound, but lost her balance and began to fall. The young girl let out a surprised scream until she was caught in someone's arms. She looked up to see that her hero was indeed the man with the curious eyes. Up close, Faye could see that Tristan's eyes weren't just brown; they had a hint of a golden color to them as well.

"I believe that's *twice* I've saved you now," he whispered with a smirk, casually grabbing the dusty frame from the young girl's slender hands. For a moment, their hands brushed against one another. Blushing slightly more than earlier, Faye slid out of his arms and stood on her own two feet to face Marcus, only to see that he wasn't alone. On either side of him were two men about the same height as Tristan, and just as well built. The one on the right had blond hair, and his eyes were as the sea; a bluish-green color. The man on the left looked more serious; he had light brown hair that was short and combed to the side. His eyes were a brilliant blue, like gems. Both of them were dressed in ivory ceremonial robes with gold trimmings.

"Faye," Marcus stated calmly, though she could detect a hint of disappointment in his voice, "allow me to introduce Kardos Starrain, High Sorcerer of Salzar," he motioned to his left, "and Ezra Clearrune, High Sorcerer of Janulai," he motioned to his right. Each of them nodded in response to their name.

Faye said nothing. Her eyes widened at the information her mind just registered. "They—they're—"

"Ah, and I see you met Tristan Belhearth," Ezra interrupted, showing a dazzling smile, "High Sorcerer of Arana."

Faye's heart skipped a beat. Slowly turning around, she glanced up at the man that saved her. His eyes didn't look curious anymore; they looked more entertained. "Hello, Faye," he whispered as he carelessly tossed the picture frame in the air. Instead if it crashing to the ground, it floated effortlessly back to its rightful spot, hanging itself up on the empty hook. "Oh, and incase you were wondering," he added as her satchel, with a flick of his wrist, magically glided from the spot Faye placed it back into her arms, "that's *my* chair I let you stand on."

Faye tried to swallow but her mouth was dry. She pieced back the events that took place, pointing at him and then the empty chair. "You're a..and I just...and you—"

"Aren't an obtuse, old and wrinkly man with a long beard," he finished her sentence, smirking at the embarrassed girl. "Sorry to disappoint you." Faye remained silent, her cheeks burning hot from embarrassment. She scolded a High Sorcerer; she told him to 'shut it'!

"Well, you certainly aren't old and wrinkly...but 'obtuse'..." Ezra chuckled.

"So, this is Faye," Kardos observed loudly, "the young Sorceress I've heard so much about." Faye didn't believe she could blush anymore than she already had. "Tell me, child...how old are you?"

47

Faye shifted her attention to him and replied softly, "Twenty-four, sir."

Ezra let out a satisfied sigh. "Only one more year until your final test," he realized. "What type of magic have you been studying?"

"Healing potions," she answered without missing a beat. "Since the...the...err," she hesitantly glanced over at Marcus who only nodded his head slightly for her to continue. "Since most of our people are in battle, some have returned hurt. Families get sick, and they don't know what medicines to take. So, I make healing potions of all kinds." Her eyes dropped to her thumbs as they fiddled with her satchel. "I've seen enough people getting hurt."

Ezra raised an eyebrow, glancing at the other High Sorcerers. "So...that's it? Nothing else but potions?" he asked in a surprised tone.

Faye glanced up at Ezra, raising an eyebrow. "Well, that's what I *mainly* study. I know how to defend myself, if that's what you're implying," she countered. For that remark, Ezra gave her another dazzling smile.

"See Tristan?" he boasted. "The people of Janulai can take care of themselves."

"It's getting late," Marcus insisted. "We should be leaving. Thank you for your time, Kardos. I trust the—situation...?"

"You have my word, Sorcerer," Kardos replied, his tone matching the serious look in his eyes. "Everything will be taken care of." He looked at Faye, his piercing blue eyes piqued with curiosity for some reason Faye couldn't fathom. "I hope our paths cross again, young Dragon Whisperer," he bowed gracefully to her and then left the room with Ezra following suit, their robes flowing behind them. Tristan followed the Sorcerers, but not before giving a small bow to Faye and Marcus, his curious eyes never leaving the young girl. Then, without saying a word, he turned on his heel and left.

"You told them?" she whispered, staring at Marcus as they walked down the empty corridor and out of Sorcerer Ezra's palace. It resided in the farthest hills of Janulai. Each Sorcerer had their own palace located in their homeland. Although they were not as extravagant as the castles of Royalty, they still showed a title of importance.

"Yes, I did. With this blood-thirsty war going on, I want to make sure you are kept safe in case—" Marcus hesitated, never finishing his thought.

"In case what?" she asked, her throat tightening as she spoke. Marcus looked into Faye's eyes and she knew something was troubling his thoughts. "Tell me what's wrong."

"It's been a long day for both of us," he stated bluntly. "Let's go home and get some rest." As they continued walking, Faye glanced down at his hand that held the walking staff. His knuckles were turning white.

She didn't bring the subject up again.

CHAPTER FOUR: LESSONS LEARNED

ALL DRAGONS ARE PART OF THE FOUR ELEMENTS: earth, fire, water, and sky."

"Naturally the sky," Faye rolled her eyes at this lesson. Marcus insisted she learn about everything at the comfort of home, instead of venturing out. "Dragons can fly."

"Not all dragons fly," Marcus corrected. "Some burrow underground and others swim. There are hundreds of dragons out in the world. Do you recall how every summer, there is a giant rainstorm when the days were at its hottest?"

"Of course I remember," Faye sighed, fidgeting with Marcus' dragon figurines carved out of wood. "The

Water Run. The Selti river fills with enough water to almost flood our lands. The stories are that the water and earth dragons worked together to make the riverbed; the earth dragons dug a path that passes through Arana, and the water dragons—well, they filled the riverbed with water. They all migrate in the summer to—I don't know, some...dragon utopia? Past Arana, past...all of this." Faye fiddled with the small sculpture more. *"At least they get to see the world,"* she thought sadly.

Faye could hear Marcus sigh as he grabbed the figurine from her hands. "There's no such thing as a—" his sentence was interrupted by a knock on the door. "For the love of—yes, yes come in!"

The door opened, and a father and son entered. The father was short and round with short, black hair. The son looked exactly like the father, but smaller in height. Part of his face was covered in a giant bloodied cloth. The father wobbled in, dragging the son behind him.

"Sorry to disturb you, Marcus," the father spoke in a gruffy, slurred voice, "but Andrew here decided to have a little adventure...*against my wishes.*" He glanced down at the child, whose head couldn't sulk any lower.

Marcus raised an eyebrow. "He did, did he?" Marcus glanced over at Faye, a small smile creeping on his face as if to say, 'I told you so'. "Well, come over here,

Andrew." He motioned for the young boy to sit by the window. Andrew trudged along, sniffling softly.

"Faye, can ya get me an ale?" the father asked. "All that walkin' made me thirsty."

"You live two huts down," she thought to herself as she gave him a small smile and curt nod.

"Hope we weren't interruptin' nothin'," the father groaned, reaching for one of the dragon carvings and using it as a tool to help scratch his cheek.

"Not at all, Declan. Faye was just having her lessons," Marcus said, examining the cut on Andrew's face. "Oh, stop blubbering, child! It's only a scratch!"

Faye returned to the table and quickly replaced the dragon carving in Declan's hand with a cup of ale. "Here you go," she said softly. As she sat down, Declan slammed the now empty cup on the table, giving a small belch of appreciation.

"Now Faye, let's skip ahead to the Cardinal Lands. The map should be on that table somewhere," Marcus suggested as he opened up a vial containing a thick, green liquid. "It smells bad, but it'll help that cut go away," he explained to Andrew as the small boy groaned in disgust.

Faye cleared her throat and glanced at the map, tracing her fingers over the mountains. "Well, there's

Salzar in the North. Hidden somewhere in Labirintas Mountains—the Mountain Maze," she looked over to Declan, who had a confused expression on his face, "is the palace of King Leonus. Salzar has control of the waterfront, and they are the ones that do a lot of trading; spices, herbs, food—"

"Weapons," Declan interrupted, looking down at his empty mug, then back at her. "What about weapons?"

Faye smiled, trying to have patience. "That's more Arana, in the South," Faye sighed, grabbing his mug and retrieving more ale. "They're near the lava pits of Kaahl."

Declan winked at Faye, causing the young girl to cringe. "'Course it is, I was just testin' ya," he raised his full glass to her with a smile as he downed the beverage once again. Faye quickly moved the map away before a large splash of ale could dampen the wording.

"Faye," Marcus called to her, "can you get me some ginger roots? Poor boy is a blubbering mess." Faye nodded once toward Marcus and hurried to the cabinet, grabbing the properly labeled jar and a bowl to crush the plant in. Sure enough, when she saw the child, he was still crying, although he wouldn't look at Faye directly. "Now, Andrew," Marcus asked as calmly as he could, "What were you doing wandering around and getting yourself hurt?"

54

"I—" the chubby boy shifted in his seat, "I was p-playing in the woods," he sniffled, "but then I—" he winced when Faye applied the new liquid to the wound. Marcus nodded towards Faye before going to take a seat with Declan.

"It's okay," Faye whispered. "This will make your face tingle a little, but that's just the herbs protecting your wound."

The boy nodded, appearing to calm down at the sound of her voice. "Thanks," he nodded.

"You're lucky, you know," Faye sighed. "The woods aren't normally this kind to strangers. I've seen the trees do worse—"

"It wasn't a stupid tree," Andrew interrupted defensively, "It was…" the boy hesitated, glancing over Faye's shoulder. Subtly, she turned around and saw Marcus and Declan having a conversation in low whispers as well. Faye looked back to Andrew and nodded for him to continue. The boy swallowed hard and took in a deep breath. "It was a dragon…I saw it! It attacked me!" he hissed when he saw Faye's look of disbelief.

"Woah, woah…calm down," Faye hushed the hysterical boy as she observed the green goop collect small pieces of bark from the wound. "It's okay."

"The dragon was huge," Andrew continued. "He was

—was as tall as the trees! His eyes were red and his belly glowed orange! He looked *right at me!* I—uh—I distracted the beast before he could eat the baker—"

"Brayden?" Marcus interrupted. "You saw Brayden in the woods?"

"Boy, you better not be tellin' one of yer lies again!" Declan warned. Faye could tell by the tone in his voice that this wasn't the first "story" Andrew has told.

"I'm telling the *truth!*" Andrew defended. "The dragon was HUGE! He saw me, growled, and started to chase me! This was from his tail!" Andrew pointed at the covered wound. "What do I have to do to make you believe me?!"

The men snickered a little and continued their hushed conversation. Faye bit her bottom lip and cautiously looked at Andrew. "You're really telling the truth? You saw a dragon?" The boy nodded silently. "I have a way for you to prove it to me. Lay down on the floor over there," Faye commanded, pointing to the floor in front of the fire pit. Andrew did as he was told as Faye hurried to the cabinets. *"I've been waiting to try this,"* Faye thought to herself excitedly. She grabbed the proper herbs, a crushing bowl, and a small mug with lukewarm water.

"Okay Andrew," Faye knelt down beside the boy, "I promise this won't hurt. This will let me into your thoughts. I'll be able to see everything you saw that night, including the dragon." She didn't know if he was being truthful about the dragon, but he gave no sign that he was making it up. Andrew nodded, a serious look on his face.

"Okay, so do I drink—"

"Not unless you want just plain water," Faye warned, taking the cup back from him. "This is for later." Andrew nodded silently, blushing a little. "Now, relax, and stop asking so many questions." She took the crushed herbs and poured it into the warm water. Muttering a few spell words, her hands began glowing green. As soon as she held onto the beverage, the contents inside the mug began to glow green as well. "Keep your eyes closed and drink this," she ordered, leading the cup towards his lips. He opened his mouth and took a gulp of the potion. As soon as he finished the drink, she held onto his hand, and muttered the spell once more.

"Recuerdos perdido."

In an instant, Faye felt the rush of air as the common area in their hut disappeared, leaving Andrew and Faye in the woods.

"My stomach," Andrew groaned. Faye looked down at the boy, and was almost sure his face turned a shade of green. "What just happened?"

"We're in your memories," Faye whispered, looking around. The trees were not their normal color, but a tint of green. Everything in the forest seemed to be greener than normal. "The spell is letting us see everything." She observed the bark, which was unnaturally green. "Damn, I used too much meadow grass. I *knew* two pinches was too much."

Andrew gulped loudly as he stood up and brushed the dirt off his clothes. "C-Can the dragon...?"

Faye shook her head. "No one can see us right now." Just then, the sound of running was heard. Faye looked behind her towards the source and could hear Andrew gasp as he saw a greener version of himself running straight through Faye.

"I'm a mighty Dragon Whisperer! Take that, Jedrek!" The greener Andrew proclaimed aloud. "HA! Your stupid Shadow people can't hurt me! I'm invincible!"

Faye looked over towards the present Andrew, who was blushing slightly. Before he could say anything, someone screamed just ahead. Faye and Andrew looked at each other and followed the sound. Once they got closer, they saw green Andy hunched behind bushes. Faye ignored the groan coming from the present Andrew as she observed what was in front of them...

A huge dragon was standing in front of a panicked baker.

"No! NO NO NO!" Brayden cried. "You—you're not supposed to be here yet! I—" he groaned in pain as he grabbed his arm.

Faye inched closer to the dragon and Brayden against Andrew's soft spoken wishes. She turned to glance at him, and saw that he mirrored the past Andrew perfectly, both having a look of terror on their faces. Faye turned back around and tried closing the space between herself and the baker. Just as she was about to peek over Brayden's shoulder, she heard a soft growl come from the dragon. She looked up and held her breath. The dragon was looking in her direction, growling softly once more. *"Can he see me?"* she thought to herself in a panic. *"I thought the spell worked...maybe more tree bark? Or not too much daisy petals? No, I did the right amount of daisy—"*

"Who's there?"

She blinked a few times, backing away quickly. Did she just—

THUD!

Faye whirled around, focused on the awkward green Andrew, who was clearly flat on his stomach. The dragon growled at the boy. Not in a menacing way, but to Faye—and she had no idea why—it sounded like he was curious. Letting out a high scream, Andrew stumbled as he stood and ran in the opposite direction. The terrified boy didn't get too far as his face unfortunately made contact with a giant tree. Brayden groaned in sympathy pain, as did Faye. She watched as present Andrew glanced at Faye, then back to the ground in embarrassment. Faye felt another rush of air as the two were back to reality, only now they were standing outside Faye's hut.

"That was...interesting," the young Sorceress muttered, thinking more about the dragon than anything else.

"You must've made that drink wrong," Andrew muttered as he stormed back into the hut, not looking back. "That's not how I remember it happening."

Faye raised an eyebrow. "You're welcome." She knew he was right, though. Everything was too green. Nevertheless, she saw a dragon, and it was in the forest. She glanced behind her, towards the direction of the woods, and knew what she had to do.

CHAPTER FIVE: THE DRAGON IN THE WOODS

FAYE WAITED UNTIL NIGHTFALL TO SNEAK OUTSIDE. Donned in her hooded green cloak, she concealed her face and headed to the forest. She knew she saw something...different... but what was it?

She followed the twists and turns of the dirt path, trying to make it to the Grandfather Tree. Although she knew the forest inside and out, it was still difficult traveling without sunlight. Luckily for Faye, there were some plants that contained a faint glow of different colors lighting the way.

"I know I saw it somewhere," she groaned as she shivered from the cold wind. Just then, she heard rustling to her right. Before she could react, someone collided with her, causing her to crash into the ground. She groaned in pain as her side ached from the fall. Faye looked up and saw the terrified eyes of Brayden Almastutter staring frantically back.

"Faye! Wh-what are you doing here?" Before she could answer, a loud hissing sound was heard throughout the forest. "Oh no," he breathed quickly, standing up and looking around. "They'll find me! Damn this forest and it's paths! I tried leaving, but I keep finding myself closer to Janulai...my wife...my childr—" a horrible shriek sounded from above. Faye looked up and saw a demon with amethyst eyes flying down towards them. "Look out, Faye!" Brayden cried, grabbing her arm and pulling her with him. "Damn myself for getting lost, and now I'm stuck with you!" he muttered to himself. Faye turned around and watched as the animal that once had wings bent and cracked as it transformed into what looked like a man, purple and black smoke rising from his body as he glared at the two runners. The demon emitted a loud shriek, causing Faye's ears to ring.

"What is that!?" Faye cried out.

"Shadow Demons. No doubt from Jedrek himself," Brayden huffed as he eventually let go of Faye's hand

and continued to run. "This way, I think....no! This way? Mother of all—" Suddenly, two Shadow Demons jumped in front of the baker, causing Brayden and Faye to skid to a stop.

"Hello, Brayden; Dragon Whisperer of Janulai," the distorted voice hissed and clicked. Faye watched as the Shadow Demon's eyes glowed a brilliant amethyst color, showing its jagged teeth as it grinned wickedly. The thing that startled Faye the most was that the Shadow Demon's mouth didn't move at all as it spoke. Just then, she felt someone grab her arm and twist it. She winced in pain as she stared back at another Shadow Demon who seemed to take interest in her right arm.

"It—It's a fire burn," she whimpered. The Shadow Demon let out a soft gurgling growl as it stared intensely at the young girl.

"No Mark," the Shadow Demon hissed, releasing his tight grip. Faye was shoved out of the way as the two Shadow Demons slowly circled around Brayden. Their backs were hunched over, and clicking noises emitted from them as their heads bobbed back and forth, as if they could smell Faye and Brayden's fear.

"P-please," he cried, "I-I'll go far away. I won't bother King Jedrek! Please! Don't h-hurt my f-family!"

he whimpered as tears streamed down his face. One of the Shadow Demons pulled Brayden close to him, his amethyst eyes inches away from the baker's face.

"*Your family...is already dead,*" it hissed. "*They suffered...*" more clicking sounds were heard as the Demon inhaled, "*until they begged me to end it. I only did as they wished. As your children wished...as your beautiful wife wished...Oh, she was in the most pain.*" A wicked smile showed sharp, razor-like teeth. Faye's heart felt like it dropped to her stomach. She saw the hurt and fear in Brayden's face multiply as he let out a wail.

"MIATH!" Brayden cried. "*MIATH!!!*" The baker screamed to the skies, his tears streaming down his face and chin. Out of nowhere, a loud roar erupted from the skies. The winds picked up fiercely as Faye looked up and couldn't believe what she saw.

A dragon. A *huge* dragon, was flying down to their spot. It's stomach glowed an orange color that rose to its neck. The dragon opened his mouth, and Faye knew that she needed to get out of the way. As soon as she did, she felt the heat of the flames crashing down to the ground. She heard the howling, demonic scream from one the Shadow Demons before it disintegrated. Faye looked up at the majestic creature as it protected the baker; its eyes glowed with a fury she had never seen before. She crawled backwards away from the ring of fire as the dragon tried protecting its master. More Shadow Demons materialized from thin air as they tried fighting off the large beast with black spears and weapons.

"Faye, Run!" Brayden cried out. "Miath protect—" suddenly, a small smoke ball struck the baker in the chest, turning to chains. Although they appeared to be smoke, they weighed Brayden down, causing him to collapse to the ground.

"Brayden!" she cried, running towards him. She jumped over the fire and hurried to the baker's side as he gasped for air. The chains wrapped tightly around his chest. Every time he moved, the chains seemed to squeeze harder. Faye heard a shriek from behind her and quickly turned around, striking a Shadow Demon with an energy ball. Her target flew towards a tree and made contact before bursting into smoke.

"F-Faye," Brayden whispered weakly, "t-tell M-Marcus..." Before he could say anything else, she felt something wrap around her waist. She looked down with enough time to see a fiery whip wrapped tightly around her before she was pulled away with a great force. She shrieked as she became airborne and crashed once more to the ground. The young Sorceress coughed and groaned in pain, but still stood her ground as her hands glowed a brilliant green.

"Such a strong Sorceress," the Shadow Demon teased. *"Someone has been training. Maybe we should find your trainer after we kill you."*

"Marcus," Faye gasped softly. She glared at the Shadow Demon and felt the energy around her grow stronger. She glanced at her hands as they glowed not green, like usual, but a brilliant purple. The Shadow Demon hissed loudly and charged forward. Faye cried aloud and punched the ground with a closed fist.

It was a feeling she never felt before.

She could literally *feel* the energy flow through her arm and into the ground, causing ripples of energy to shoot out. The Shadow Demon flew through the air and, before colliding into a tree, teleported himself back to the ground and growled at Faye.

Faye wobbled for a moment. All of a sudden she was exhausted. The Shadow Demon close to the baker stared at Faye and hesitated for a moment.

"Maruto, there is only one I know...who can do that." he hissed.

"That filthy Varjo!" Maruto screamed. *"Da'Kunya, take the Dragon Whisperer to the Realm,"* the Demon hissed. He then glared at Faye, unleashing his whip

once more with a crack. Faye dodged the attack successfully, shooting an energy ball at the Shadow Demon, but just grazing his leg. He flinched in pain. *"You will tell us what you know, Sorceress. You will tell us about Jaako's location."* Faye raised an eyebrow at the unfamiliar name. *"Do it, or—"* Out of the corner of her eye, she saw Miath's tail circle around, making contact with the Shadow Demon. The dragon faced Faye and roared.

"RUN!"

Faye hesitated for a moment, believing to be imagining things...did he roar? Or did he talk?

Miath tilted his head and for a moment, time stood still. They stared at each other for what seemed like an eternity before a Shadow Demon climbed onto Miath's neck, wrapping it in the same chains as the Baker. This was able to bring Faye back to reality as she ran for her life.

She ran through the trees and shrubbery, not caring about the noise she made...not caring who could hear her as she cried loudly. She fell to the ground once out of the forest, turning back in time to hear Miath's roar one last time.

"FAYE!"

There it was again. There was no doubt in her mind

that someone was calling her name. Was it the dragon? Could she...?

Suddenly, someone grabbed her shoulder. She looked up, and didn't know if it was relief or guilt passing through her mind as Marcus glared down at her.

***

"I've been looking everywhere for you," Marcus yelled once they were back home. "You know the risks! You could have—"

"Why didn't you tell me about the baker?!" Faye snapped. "What else are you hiding from me?!"

Marcus seemed taken aback for a moment. "Faye," he sighed tiredly, rubbing his forehead, "No one knows about you. No one knows about your Gift. Think of what could happen if they did! The baker's wife is a known gossiper! She can't keep anything a secret," he hissed. "Imagine if she knew your secret. *Our* secret! The Shadow Demons won't just come after you...they could come after me as well!" Faye looked down to the floor, knowing Marcus was right. She remembered what the Shadow Demon told Brayden in the forest.

"They suffered..."

"FAYE!" Marcus slammed his fist on the table. "This is serious! They know who you are now!"

"Yes, but they didn't take me! The one named Da Kun-eya said 'no Mark'," the young girl imitated the gravelly voice, "and let me go." Marcus hesitated, looking at Faye as if he saw a ghost.

"What did you say? You got a name?" Marcus asked, more intrigued.

Faye nodded. "Yes. Da Kun-eya?" she hesitated, trying to pronounce the name.

"*Da'Kunya,*" Marcus whispered. "Faye, what else happened? Did you hear any other names?"

Faye bit her bottom lip as she thought back. "Yes. There was a name they asked me about.. Jako? Jaah-ko? I can't remember how he said it exactly, but he looked at me as if I were to know. That's when Miath swung his tail at him, and…" Faye hesitated. *He spoke to me. Say it, Faye!* "And…I ran. That's it." she lied. Faye saw how scared Marcus was; no need to panic him any more.

"Well," Marcus cleared his throat, "As long as you are safe." He began fidgeting with his cane, tapping on one of the diamonds repeatedly. "It's late," he cleared his throat once more. "You should get to bed." In one swift movement, he wrapped Faye in a tight hug. "I'm glad you're alright. I love you so much." He pulled away from

69

the hug and smiled at the young Sorceress.

"I love you too," she replied.

"You know you've always been like a daughter to me, Faye. Your mom and dad—" he blinked away tears as his lip trembled. He wrapped her in another tight hug. "They would be so...*so* proud of you." There was silence for a while, until Marcus cleared his throat for a third time and headed to his room.

No words were said. No words needed to be said. There was a mutual family love that lingered in the main room for a while. Faye smiled to herself as she headed to her room. She felt so lucky to have someone as caring as Marcus. *I wonder if that's what my father would have been like,* she thought to herself, then she shook her head.

No one was like Marcus...and she wouldn't have it any other way.

CHAPTER SIX: THE AMETHYST EYES

SHE WAS RUNNING THROUGH THE FOREST. Her dreams usually were a tad intense, but this wasn't like normal dreams. She truly felt fear coursing through her veins as she ran for dear life. Something was chasing her. Faye had no idea what it was, but all of her instincts were telling her that she only had two choices: run or die. The young Sorceress formed balls of pure energy with her hands and threw them behind her, catching a glimpse of the purple and black smoke swirls closely gaining on her. Her legs were becoming tired and her lungs burned as she gasped for air. Something suddenly caught her foot and she fell to the ground. However, instead of hitting the dirt and leaves, she hit cold marble.

Faye quickly stood up and observed her surroundings; red and gold patterned tapestries were everywhere, and the marble was cold against her bare feet. She looked around for the mysterious smoke, only to find statues of knights standing at attention on either side of the hallway and torches hanging on the walls, illuminating the area. She wandered into another room, again surrounded by colors of red and gold. Standing alone by a window was a man. He looked old and tired. Quietly, she walked behind him and gazed out his window. Judging by the view of mountains, Faye knew she wasn't in Janulai.

Her thoughts were interrupted by the man's violent cough. In desperation, he covered his mouth with his silk kerchief. Faye's eyes widened as she saw specks of red dotting the delicate silk. This man was sick, and from the looks of him, he didn't have much time. Exhaustion and sadness covered the man's face like a veil. He ran his fingers through his brown and gray speckled hair and called out for a guard.

"Find me the Sorcerer and Princess. I'd like to have words," he asked calmly. Faye raised an eyebrow and looked around the room once more. This wasn't just any ordinary man.

This was a King. And he was dying.

Faye searched through her mind, trying to

remember who this King could be. Red and gold tapestries...mountains... *"King Leonus,"* she thought to herself in realization. *"This is Salzar."* As the King continued to cough, she hurried to the doors, desperate to leave. She couldn't stand seeing him die; even if she never met him before, the pain of seeing someone leave their loved ones...it was all too familiar to her. She attempted to grab the doorknob, only to witness her hand passing through, as if she was nothing more than a shadow.

She heard movement behind the door. Instinctively taking a step back, the doors swung open and revealed Kardos. He was dressed in his ceremonial garments, like the first time they met. The High Sorcerer walked through her, which sent a cold sensation through her body. Just then, Kardos shivered, turning around to face her direction. The young girl froze. Did he feel that, too? But...it was just a dream...

"Kardos, we must discuss the future of this Kingdom," the King said softly, turning Faye's attention once more to the sick King.

The High Sorcerer nodded, turning back to the King. "Yes, King Leonus. With your daughter's," he cleared his throat, "betrothed arriving soon," Faye could hear the disapproval in his voice, "we need to prepare for his arrival."

"Yes, sple—" the King was once again interrupted by a coughing fit, this one worse than the last.

Faye couldn't stay in that room anymore. She walked through the door, but instead of being back in the cold hallway she found herself in another room. Unlike the last room which was filled with warm colors of red and gold, this room was cold as ice and was decorated in black silk that covered the windows, a few paintings, and the canopy of a rather large bed. Standing next to the bed was a woman, gazing down at a body lying on the bed. Chills ran through Faye's entire body.

The dream suddenly felt very real.

The frigid air in the room made the hair on Faye's arms stand. She heard the soft whispers echoing through the walls from voices unknown. Faye inched closer to the bed, tears filling her eyes as she gazed upon the still, forever sleeping body of King Leonus. Even in death, the old King looked exhausted; as if he was cursed to never find peace, even in the afterlife.

The room grew deathly still. In that moment, Faye felt someone's presence close to her. Slowly, the young girl turned around. The woman that was standing silently in the room now stood inches away from Faye. The woman's eyes were like glowing amethysts, filled with a power unlike anything the young Sorceress had ever felt before.

All Faye wanted to do now was wake up.

It wasn't that she was scared of the strange woman staring at her through glowing eyes, but because of what she said:

"Hello, Dragon Whisperer."

Faye felt something take hold of her ankle and throw her as if she was nothing more than a rag doll. The young Sorceress crashed into a tree and hit the ground hard enough for the wind to be knocked out of her. She gasped for air as she tried to stand up and face her predator. She saw nothing but a storm of purple and black smoke as she found herself back in the forest. Faye felt fear coursing through her body as she attempted to throw energy balls at the smoke, unable to slow it down. Just when she was being engulfed in the dark clouded mass, she heard a mighty roar.

CHAPTER SEVEN: THE ALTERCATION

FAYE WOKE UP, COVERED IN SWEAT. Her heart was beating as fast as the wings of a hummingbird. This felt too real to be a coincidence.

Someone knew who she was; worse than that, someone knew *what* she was.

Rummaging around her somewhat tidy room until she found her green cloak, she quickly got dressed and headed into the small common area in their hut. Marcus was known to be awake first in the morning, but he was nowhere to be seen. She peered down the small corridor that led to his bedroom and saw that the door was shut.

"He must still be asleep. I'll tell him everything later," she thought to herself. Just then, her stomach growled softly. She hadn't eaten since yesterday's soup, which she never told Zachariah or Marcus for fear of their overprotective traits dominating the day. Faye grabbed her satchel and headed to the village, knowing the perfect place for breakfast.

***

The Hoof of Pig tavern was the best place to get a full meal at a fair price. Faye enjoyed her warm porridge with an egg on the side and a glass of goat's milk, listening to the ambience of the Tavern; the chatter of customers, the clanking of dishes and chairs, and the normal bustle of crowds coming in and out.

"Anythin' else I can get for ya, darlin'? You look like ya haven't eaten in days!" the Tavern Keeper, Little Verna (who was actually taller than most men) asked as she cleaned off the table next to Faye.

"Thank you, Little Verna, but I'm okay. I am actually expecting my friend to join me soon, but I don't—"

"I'll have what she is having, thank you." a voice said from behind the young girl. Faye whirled around, surprised to see not her huntsman friend, but the curious High Sorcerer in his regular garments. Giving Little Verna a small yet charming smile, Tristan sat adjacent to the shocked Faye.

"Not your usual friend, there! This one is actually goin' to be orderin'!" Little Verna chuckled as she hurried into the kitchen.

"What are you doing here?" Faye asked in hushed tones.

Tristan looked around, raising an eyebrow. "I...I'm ordering breakfast. This is the Hoof of Pig Tavern, is it not?"

Faye glared at the High Sorcerer. "You're in my friend's seat. He should be here any moment," she warned.

Tristan's eyes lit up. "Ah! The more, the merrier! Miss! Please! We need an extra chair," he motioned to Little Verna as she carried over his food.

"Hang on! I only got two arms!" she grumbled. "You know, I might have liked your other friend better, Faye...he was quiet," she winked playfully at the High Sorcerer as she brought the third chair over. Faye couldn't help but smile at the remark as she watched Little Verna walk away.

"So, have you received it yet?" Tristan asked, taking in a spoonful of porridge.

The young girl raised an eyebrow. "Received what?"

"Your Mark."

Faye's eyes widened and she quickly glanced around to make sure no one else was listening. When she was sure that the conversation between the two of them was free of eavesdroppers, she sighed. "No, not yet."

"It'll hurt like hell," he continued, focused more on eating than on the girl. "It'll feel like your skin is burning and you can't relieve the pain, no matter what you do. Of course, you can't even get near water without losing your power temporarily—"

"How do you know that?" Faye asked, shocked at his expertise on the subject.

Tristan shrugged. "I have my ways," he said casually. When Faye continued to glare at the High Sorcerer, he sighed annoyingly. "It is the job of the High Sorcerers to know everything about everyone wanting to be a High Sorcerer, that's all. So, relax."

"Hard to relax when someone knows more than they should," a voice challenged. Faye looked behind her to see Zachariah. Although she could not see his whole face, his angry eyes glared at Tristan.

"Why does everyone want to be behind me?" Faye muttered to herself. "Zachariah," she said in a normal tone, "this is Tristan Belhearth, High Sorcerer of Arana.

Tristan, this is Zachariah; my truest friend and Huntsman to—"

"The Elven Clan," Tristan finished. "Like I said," he shrugged his shoulders, "we know everything. Besides, we met earlier yesterday."

Zachariah took his seat, still glaring at Tristan. "I will give you the kindness of common courtesy, since you seem to be an acquaintance of Faye's," Zachariah stated, "but don't mistake that courtesy for trust."

Tristan raised his hands in defeat. "Fair enough, Huntsman." Faye and Tristan ate in silence for a little while when Zachariah finally broke the silence.

"Faye, you seem troubled."

Faye looked at Zachariah guiltily, then away from his concerned eyes. "Just couldn't sleep. Had this...this weird dream. I wanted to talk to Marcus about it first, but he—"

"Marcus arrived at the High Sorcerer's tower requesting an audience this morning." Tristan said through a mouthful of food. Faye stared at him, her mouth ajar. "Now before you bombard me with questions," he paused to take a swig from his drink, then cleared his throat, "he requested the audience alone, so I was asked to leave... so no, I do not know what was discussed."

"And here I thought you knew everything," Zachariah commented, an obvious tone of disdain in his voice.

"I know what I need to know in order to survive, *Elf*," Tristan snapped back. "All your kind knows is how to run and hide when truly needed."

Zachariah slammed his fist down on the table, causing more than a few townsfolk to stare at the huntsman curiously while others shook their head in disapproval.

"Wait," Faye interrupted. "You mean to say Marcus is there now?"

"Quite possibly," he replied, his challenging eyes never leaving Zachariah.

Faye stood from the table. Reaching into her satchel, she grabbed the money for her food, placed it on the table and headed out the door without looking back.

"Faye, wait!" She could hear Zachariah call out to her, but she didn't stop. She had to see Marcus; she had to tell him about the dream, tell him about those eyes...those cold, amethyst eyes that burned into Faye's memory.

"Did you hear what I said?" Zachariah's voice grew more concerned, bringing Faye back to the present. She glanced up at Zachariah, shaking her head. "I said 'think about what you're doing'. He might want to have this meeting alone for a reason," he warned. Before Faye could reply, a terrified scream was heard throughout the marketplace.

"Thief! Stop him!" the voice cried out. Crashing through the crowd was a stranger dressed in a dark purple cloak carrying a leather pouch. Before running past, the stranger momentarily locked eyes with Faye.

The young girl's heart skipped a beat. Everything felt as if time slowed down, for staring back into her own green eyes were the glowing amethyst eyes of a man with a shadowed face and a challenging smile.

"Those eyes," she whispered as he ran past. Without hesitating, Faye followed the thief into the forest with the huntsman closely behind. The thief weaved back and forth through the forest with amazing agility. Faye was closing the gap, launching energy balls at the thief until one successfully struck the stranger's leg. As he fell, the thief threw the pouch into the air and disappeared. Faye stared in shock at the once occupied spot as it was now covered in purple and black smoke.

"Faye," Zachariah called out. She glanced over towards him and then followed his gaze.

Faye knew she was chasing one stranger into the

forest. Now, six strangers, all with dark purple hooded robes on, surrounded the two.

All of their eyes were glowing amethyst.

"At last we finally meet." They all spoke at once, yet their voice sounded as if one person was actually speaking. The voice sounded distorted and unfamiliar, a feeling that made Faye uncomfortable. A ring of purple and black fire soon surrounded them all.

"Shadow Demons," Faye gasped softly.

"Who are you?! What do you want?!" Zachariah called out to the hooded strangers as they slowly crept towards the two.

"We are part of the greater plan. We are the New World, sent to rid the memory of old. We are the Shadow Realm, and we are here for her," the six strangers pointed to Faye simultaneously.

Zachariah stood in front of Faye defensively. "You will have to go through me first, and I shall send you back to the Realms once more."

The strangers were suddenly still. Their eyes stopped glowing. Faye glanced around the motionless circle of the Shadow Realm. "Wh-What do you want with me?!" she asked. Fear coursed through her veins and her heart was beating faster than her mind could follow. After a few moments of stillness, their eyes burst back to life, obtaining the amethyst shine once again. Their hands glowed and the circle of fire grew.

"We want your Gift, Dragon Whisperer."

"Faye, look out!" Zachariah called out, shoving the young girl out of the way to dodge a blast of dark purple fire. When Faye stood her ground, she glanced over at her friend who had already retrieved his twin silver daggers from the sides of his boots, spinning them around and striking an enemy. Faye struck one with an energy ball, but it wasn't enough. The Shadow Demon soon conjured a long metal spear out of smoke. It glowed with a vengeance, and Faye knew she was in trouble. The Shadow Demon glared at her with determination in his eyes and lunged forward. Weaponless, Faye continued throwing energy balls at the stranger, who struck them with his spear, causing them to crash into the ground and multiple trees. The stranger swung his spear and made contact with Faye, knocking her to the ground. She gasped for air, but didn't have a chance to breathe as the stranger swung at her again. Faye instinctively rolled to the right, just missing contact.

"Think, Faye..think!" she thought to herself in a panic. Glancing over to Zachariah, she saw him in mid-air as he threw one of his daggers directly at someone. The stranger fell to the ground and disappeared in smoke,

leaving the dagger behind. Reaching into her satchel, she grabbed a small vial that contained blue liquid and hurled it toward her opponent. He caught it in one hand and chuckled softly.

"Dragon Whisperer, you are not as difficult of a challenge as we thought," he taunted as he crushed the vial in his fist. Faye smiled defiantly. In an instant, the stranger was engulfed in a blazing blue flame, which he tried patting out but it only grew with each movement he made. He ran for a few short moments until he disappeared in smoke as well.

"Faye, run!" Zachariah called out. Looking towards the source of the call, she saw her friend running towards her with what seemed like twice as many Shadow Realm opponents as just a few moments ago. Taking her friend's advice, she ran, throwing a large energy ball towards the purple fire that surrounded them. It gave them enough of a gap to jump through before the flames returned.

"Every time I struck one down, two more took their place!!" Zachariah commented, running by her side.

"How many did you strike down?!" Faye asked, glancing back at the strangers from the Shadow Realm who ran straight through their own barrier, untouched by the flames.

"Four...at first. Then three more after," he admitted.

"You couldn't stop at just the one?" she snapped. Suddenly, a burning pain coursed through Faye's right leg, causing her to fall and scream in agony. She looked down and saw the purple and black fire around her leg. It felt as if it was digging into her skin in desperation. She clawed against the flames in her own desperation, tears streaming down her face. She felt Zachariah lift her and run with her in his arms.

"It burns! Zachar—" the flame grew darker as she felt the burning sensation begin the slowly course through the inside of her leg. She let out another scream of agony.

"Stay with me, Faye! You'll be alright," she barely heard his reassuring words as she continued to fade in and out of consciousness from the pain. Just then, there was a roar.

And then everything went black.

CHAPTER EIGHT: THE DRAGON

S HE WAS SURROUNDED BY FIRE. There wasn't an end to the flames. Faye searched for an opening, but the ring of fire began to close around her. She looked around in confusion and panic. The flames were large and getting closer, but why wasn't she feeling the warmth?

Soon, Faye was completely engulfed in flames. Her robe, hands, and legs were caught on fire, and yet it didn't hurt. She observed her hands, taking note of the flames dancing across her fingertips. It felt nothing like fire should. Faye looked down and the flames were flowing all across her body as if time had slowed around her. The flames suddenly began burning brighter until there was a blinding flash.

It was now night. Faye observed her hands and the rest of her body and noticed the flames were gone. Just then, she heard a blood-curdling scream just ahead where there was a brilliant glow. She ran towards the sound and soon regretted it.

It was her hut. Her hut was on fire.

This wasn't Marcus' hut, though. She remembered this vividly, just not from this vantage point; seeing the young girl cry in desperation as village folk tried their best to extinguish the purple fire engulfing the house, seeing a younger version of Marcus grab the young girl who tried fighting him off in a crazy attempt to run into the burning house. Her heart sank as her mind finally grasped the situation.

That little girl was Faye seventeen years ago. This was her memory of her parents' death.

Her eyes filled with tears as she observed the tragic scene. No one knew where the purple fire came from, and no one could save her mother and father from the flames.

Marcus cried as he held young Faye. "Why?! Why?!"

This was a question that still haunted Faye, even seventeen years later. Suddenly, she felt a burning sensation coursing through her back. She screamed as she arched upwards in pain, squeezing her eyes shut as the burning sensation caused her to fall backwards. She rolled around, trying to rid herself of the pain, but to no avail. When she opened her eyes she was once again engulfed in the strange flames.

"I am here, little Dragon Whisperer," a low voice called out in her mind. She wasn't even sure it was a voice, more like a feeling in her soul. Suddenly, she felt a strange, calming sensation and decided to lie still as the flames continued to dance along her skin, burning nowhere else but her back. The pain was unbearable, but she remained still.

There was another blinding light....

***

When she opened her eyes, things began to focus slowly. She saw Zachariah, armed with his twin daggers, fear and anger in his eyes.

"Zachariah?" she asked, her voice scratchy. "Wha—"

Just then, there was a soft growl. Swallowing hard, she slowly looked up and gazed upon a set of brilliant yellow eyes. They blinked and showed concern. She scrambled to her feet and took a few steps back.

The dragon rose, its dark green scales blending in

with the forest scenery around them. When the sunlight hit the scales on its back, they appeared to be a brighter green than what they were, while the scales on its underbelly were a lighter yellow. The dragon's large tail had two spikes on either side, and it moved slowly behind the dragon as it walked.

"Get behind me, Faye!" Zachariah warned the girl as he took a defensive stance. The dragon glared at the huntsman and bared its teeth, letting out a threatening growl.

Faye gasped softly as she felt a feeling of protection overwhelm her. She quickly moved between the two and raised her hands in the air as if that alone would protect the dragon from any harm. "No, Zachariah! Don't! He won't hurt me!" she pleaded. She looked back at the dragon, its eyes still glaring at Zachariah. "It's okay, dragon..." she explained as the dragon shifted its attention from the huntsman to the girl. Hesitantly, she extended her hand to try and touch the scales on the dragon's chest. "He is rather protective of me, but he means well, and I assure you no one will harm you."

The dragon let out a snort and lowered his head until Faye was looking directly into the dragon's large eyes. She tilted her head slightly in similarity to the dragon's movement, curiosity rushing through her mind. Then, very slowly, Faye placed her hand on the bridge of his nose. The scales felt smooth and leathery, like her satchel whenever she'd trace her fingers along the edges. When the dragon closed his eyes, Faye's mind seemed to overflow with images of herself collapsed on the ground. Then the view shifted until she saw the strangers from the Shadow Realm, panic written on their faces as they disappeared quickly in purple and black smoke.

When the view shifted back to the young unconscious girl, she heard a soft growl rise from what felt like inside herself. Suddenly, there was a loud battle cry resounding throughout the forest. The view changed once again and Faye was now seeing Zachariah charging at full speed, armed with his twin daggers.

It was then she realized that she was seeing everything from the dragon's point of view.

With a simple flick of the dragon's green tail, he sent Zachariah flying into a tree. The view shifted back to the girl who seemed to be writhing in pain. Faye could see her back arch and the sweat on her brow, and frowned.

"This must be why Zachariah and Marcus worry so much," she thought to herself, feeling a twinge of guilt.

The dragon curled up behind young girl as if to

comfort her, nuzzling the side of Faye's head as she groaned in pain.

"I am here, little Dragon Whisperer," a voice echoed in her mind again.

Removing her hand from the dragon's scaly touch, Faye began breathing quickly, looking from Zachariah to the tree he made impact with and then back to the dragon, who only nodded slowly.

"His voice," she uttered softly. "He just—it was—I just—*saw*—through his eyes." Faye looked at Zachariah who was now by her side. How he moved so fast and silently, she would have never known. "It happened just now, when I touched him...he showed me what happened when I was—" she sucked in air quickly as she felt a burning sensation in her back.

"Faye? Faye, what is it?" Zachariah asked. She felt his hand awkwardly touch the middle of her back as he tried to comfort her.

"My back," she groaned. "It burns!" Without thinking, she began taking off her green hooded robe until she was only dressed in her white blouse and pants.

"Let me see," Zachariah insisted. Faye heard a low growl from the dragon, and couldn't help but roll her eyes at the action.

"He's a friend, dragon," she assured loudly, feeling a sense of hostility for some reason. She could feel Zachariah's fingers as he carefully lowered the top of the blouse. A cool breeze of air struck the area that burned, letting Faye feel a bit of relief if only for a moment.

She waited for Zachariah to say something. There was silence. He let go of the shirt and gasped.

"Witchcraft," he uttered softly, a hint of panic in his voice.

Faye became fearful. Had the black and purple smoke poisoned her skin? Was she dying? she slid her fingers under the top of her blouse and felt the rough, scaly skin.

"If you think it's witchcraft, then you *are* dense," a voice challenged. Turning around, she saw Tristan standing behind Zachariah.

The High Sorcerer smirked at Faye as he walked towards her. "By the way, thanks for leaving me at the tavern with Little Verna...I would rather meet your dragon than carry another conversation with her any day."

"If it is not witchcraft, *Sorcerer*," there was a tone of frustration in the huntsman's voice, "then what is it?"

Faye locked eyes with Tristan as he ignored her

friend. He motioned for the young girl to turn around. Faye obliged, facing Zachariah. Even though she could not see the huntsman's entire face, his eyes were like the daggers still in his hands: cold and aimed at Tristan. "I won't hurt you," Tristan reassured Faye. "You know this, and so does your dragon."

"M-my dragon? Well, wha—?"

"I *need* to see your back." Tristan's voice was calm and soothing. His touch was warm yet light as a feather, as if one was being delicate with glass. The cool breeze once again brushed against her skin, easing the pain just slightly. "Congratulations, Faye Haybear," Tristan said as he lifted her shirt back up, "you have your Mark. Now you have to leave home."

CHAPTER NINE: THE SPELL

The words hung in the air like a thick blanket of fog.

"I—I have to leave? When?" Faye asked as Zachariah cleared his throat and handed back her hooded green robe. Blushing slightly, she thanked her friend and re-dressed herself in her green garments, concealing her normal clothes once again. The young girl then turned to face Tristan and met his back. She walked around until their eyes locked. "Tristan! When?!"

If his eyes showed guilt, Faye did not see it. "You have to leave now."

When the words finally hit her, Faye didn't know if she preferred this hit or the one she took from the Shadow Realm. "Now?" she whispered. "Well, can I just—"

"Dammit Faye, NO!" Tristan yelled. "It's too risky!

Soon, Jedrek will have his lackeys track you down. Why do you think there are no Dragon Whisperers wandering out and about? He's capturing them all, killing them off or torturing them for all we know." Faye recalled the burning sensation her leg endured and shuddered at the thought of what else could have happened.

"You mean the Shadow Realm, don't you?" Zachariah asked, concealing his daggers in his boots once again.

Faye noticed Tristan's body tense. "What do you know of the Shadow Realm, Elf?" he asked coldly.

"They were here," Zachariah replied in the same tone, "trying to take her. Saying that they wanted her Gift." The huntsman looked back at Faye, and his gaze softened. "They called her 'Dragon Whisperer', like they already knew. It appeared as if they knew for a long time."

Tristan let out a yell of frustration and cursed to the skies. Faye had never seen anyone this upset. She looked at the dragon, the only quiet thing in the forest, as he silently stared back at Faye, his yellow eyes large with curiosity.

"We have to go," Tristan ordered. "We have to go see Kardos; he has to know about this. Faye, get on your dragon with Zachariah. I'll meet you there."

Faye shook her head in shock and disbelief. "We don't have to get there by dragon. High Sorcerer Ezra's tower is just—" Without any warning, Tristan grabbed Faye by the waist and hoisted her up on the dragon's back.

"I never said the meeting was taking place in Janulai, did I?" Tristan challenged, his eyes showing anger rather than the curiosity from their first encounter. Faye glanced at Zachariah, his eyes filled with shock at Tristan's actions. "Don't make me do the same to you, huntsman. I'm in no mood," he warned softly. Remaining silent, Zachariah easily climbed onto the dragon's back, securely holding onto Faye.

"Well then, where are we going?" she asked.

"You'll be heading to Salzar, the mountain Kingdom in the North," Tristan answered.

It took a moment for Faye to understand what was happening. For the first time in her twenty-four years, she was leaving Janulai and had no idea when she could return.

"Faye!" Tristan interrupted her thoughts. "Now is not the time to hesitate! Go to Salzar, NOW!" His voice was full of determination and authority. She looked from Zachariah to the dragon's back, not knowing if the

Dragon could even understand her.

"Okay, dragon...we need to go to Salzar. Do you know how to get—" Without warning, the dragon expanded its wings and with one effortless movement, they were already in the clouds.

The view was breathtaking. She ignored the feeling of her heart jumping up to her throat and realized just how vast and large the forest of Janulai really was. Faye looked ahead and admired the snowy mountaintops that peeked past the clouds, ignoring the short strands of her red hair whipping around her face as the cool air greeted the travelers.

"You were right after all, Zachariah!" Faye called out above the wind.

"With what?" he asked.

"Once I have my dragon, I really *can* travel!" she laughed. Faye didn't mind that she was the only one laughing, even though she imagined Zachariah smirking a little. She observed the large green dragon, admiring the beautiful yet intricate design on his wings. When the sunlight danced on the scales, they seemed to shimmer as they changed back and forth from green to yellow, reminding her of the meadows she would play in when she was just a little girl.

"Does your dragon have a name?" Zachariah

inquired. Faye frowned, realizing she had no idea if the dragon had a name yet or not.

"What should I call you, I wonder? Do you even have a name?" Faye thought to herself as she traced her fingers along the scales on the dragon's back. Just then, she felt an overwhelming feeling, followed by a voice echoing in her mind.

"Rinji," the voice said. It was deep, and soothing to hear.

Faye looked around in a panic. "Rinji?" she repeated out loud.

"Rinji, huh? That's an odd name," Zachariah commented. "However, it isn't *my* dragon I suppose." His voice had a hint of amusement before he quickly gripped tighter onto Faye.

Faye became suddenly confused. *"That voice,"* she thought to herself, *"it sounds so..."*

"Familiar?" the voice interrupted her thoughts. *"Well, it should. I called to you a few days ago. You and your huntsman friend were leaving the forest with your clovers. You turned, and I had hoped you spotted me, but—"*

Faye let out a gasp. "This is so strange," she said.

"What is?" Zachariah asked, concern in his voice.

Faye let out a short chuckle. "I think the air is getting to me...I thought the dragon—"

"I thought I told you my name is Rinji," the voice corrected. To verify, the dragon let out a soft growl.

Faye's eyes widened. "He can talk," she whispered. "Zachariah, did you hear him?" she asked in wonder. She turned to face her friend, only to receive an odd stare.

"Faye...I didn't hear anything." Just then, there was a distant roar that caused Zachariah to turn around. Faye, however, was only focused on the low voice echoing in her mind.

"No one can understand me but you, little one. I knew it was you I was supposed to be with from the moment I saw you under the Grandfather Tree. I have waited a millennia to find you, though I imagined, well hoped, for someone a little older," Rinji confessed.

"Faye, look!" Zachariah called. When she turned around, she couldn't believe what she saw. Soon flying next to them was a beautiful red dragon, slightly larger than Rinji. When the sunlight hit the vibrant red scales, it seemed as if the dragon itself was on fire.

The one thing that shocked Faye was not just the dragon, but the person seen riding it.

"This is Nuria," Tristan introduced, petting the side of the red dragon. "She was born in the lava pits of Kaahl, and she is my dragon."

Faye's eyes widened. No wonder he knew so much about the Dragon Whisperers' Mark and the pain one would have to bear when receiving it. Tristan Belhearth, High Sorcerer of Arana, was a Dragon Whisperer.

"You're a Dragon Whisperer, too?! Why didn't you say anything back at the tavern?!" Faye asked.

"Careful, Faye," Rinji's voice echoed in her mind as a feeling of caution coursed through her body. *"Something tells me this isn't a conversation we should get into just yet."*

Tristan's face grew solemn. "I had my reasons," he snapped. She followed his line of sight and found herself staring at the huntsman, whose expression mirrored Tristan's perfectly. There was an obvious tension in the skies, and it made Faye uncomfortable. "Follow me," he instructed quickly. Without saying another word, he jumped off Nuria's back, leaving Zachariah and Faye staring in awe.

"He's mad!" Zachariah shouted. "Absolutely mad!" Over their heads, Nuria swooped above them, letting out a loud hiss.

"Blasted female," Rinji growled. Faye was confused, glancing from Nuria to Rinji.

"What is it?!" Faye thought, eyeing the red dragon.

"She wants you to jump," Rinji insisted. Sure enough,

the red dragon continued to swoop lower, her wings inches from the top of Faye's head.

"Jump!"

Faye gasped softly. Did—did Nuria..??

"Your Sorcerer friend wouldn't let you jump to your death, but still..." Rinji growled again, baring his teeth to Nuria. *"I can sense your fear, little one. I won't let anything happen to you, and it seems neither will these two human men."*

Faye blushed immediately. *"He can sense my feelings...how did I forget that?!"* she thought to herself.

"Don't forget we can communicate by thoughts as well, little one," Rinji reminded thoughtfully. She began to think of her options. There was a spell she remembered reading off one of Marcus' papers in his hut, but it was in Elvish. *"It could work,"* Rinji replied in her mind. She felt the feeling of reinforcement and encouragement as the words entered her subconscious. Faye balance carefully on Rinji's back.

"We can jump from here, Rinji," Faye instructed. *"I know what to do."*

"Faye!" Zachariah called in a panic, "are you mad?! Let your dragon—"

"Don't you think Tristan would have just landed with *his* dragon? He wouldn't just let us fall to our

102

death," Faye explained, grabbing for Zachariah's hand.

"How can you trust him?! You barely know him!" Zachariah challenged.

She looked him in the eye with determination. "Do you trust *me?*" she asked simply. Zachariah's brow furrowed in confusion and then realization reflected in his eyes. He *did* trust her. She knew he always would. He grabbed onto her hand, but Faye pulled the huntsman close to her. "Don't let go, no matter what!" she ordered right before the two jumped off of Rinji's back.

The wind was whipping around them as the two began their fast descent. Faye closed her eyes and began reciting the spell she remembered. She focused on herself and Zachariah, holding onto his waist tighter. She visualized them protected by the air circling around them and easily carrying the two safely.

"Faye," she heard Zachariah gasp in awe. "Open your eyes." When she finally did, she couldn't help but smile. Surrounding them was a small cyclone carrying the two safely to the ground where Tristan was waiting. She saw his brown eyes look up at them in amazement and smiled.

"I didn't know you knew the *Flauga* enchantment... that dates back to the early Elven Clan ages." Zachariah laughed. She looked back up at his partially covered face, his dark eyes glimmering and squinting. She imagined him smiling through his silk scarf and couldn't help but smile back.

"*Flauga,*" she recited perfectly. "The flight spell...I'm glad you approve," she beamed, "Marcus taught that to me." Just then, out of nowhere, Zachariah embraced her in a tight hug. In that instant, Faye could feel the difference in that one embrace. This was more than just one of protection. "*Maybe he's accepting magic after all,*" she thought to herself.

"*Don't count on it, little one,*" Rinji's voice echoed in her mind. "*He's probably just relieved to be on the ground once more.*" Faye laughed softly, unsure whether it was at the fact that she could still communicate with Rinji from a distance or at Zachariah's secret fear of heights.

"We'll make an Elf out of you yet," Zachariah teased as he released her from his embrace.

"Now that you are done hugging," Tristan interrupted, "can we proceed?"

Faye looked around the mountain area and saw nothing but rocks; that, as well as dirt, snow, and cold winds seemed to mainly occupy the area. Faye was surprised at the sudden change of weather, and already missed the warm sun in Janulai. Although her hooded robe was warm, it wasn't quite warm enough.

"Tristan," she shivered slightly, "I don't see any path that we can—" she looked at the High Sorcerer's hands and grew silent. They not only glowed a beautiful red, but it was as if fire danced slowly around his skin. He walked towards Faye and grabbed her hands. Gasping softly, she stared at the flames as they intertwined between their hands. Faye stared up at Tristan, who was already staring at her. His brown eyes were lit with excitement. She noticed the hint of gold in his eyes once again and blushed.

"Well done with the *Flauga* enchantment," he whispered softly, winking at the young Sorceress before walking away. Faye blushed slightly and watched as he silently did the same thing to Zachariah's hands. She looked down at her own and admired the beauty of the flames as they danced around her hands and kept them warm. Testing a theory, she placed a palm on the side of her face and was welcomed with the touch of warmth. Sure enough, as she moved her hand away the warmth disappeared slowly, but no burn was left on her face.

"Where exactly are we going?" Faye broke the silence, still staring at her hands. "There doesn't seem to be a path anywhere."

"Kardos is a very private person," Tristan explained. "If the path to his tower was visible to everyone, he wouldn't be so mysterious." Walking past Faye, he looked around at their surroundings, touching large rocks as he past them. "Here it is!" Tristan exclaimed. Faye followed Tristan and gasped.

In front of them was a narrow footpath alongside the mountain's steep side. It seemed to go on for miles.

"I stand corrected; *this* is madness!" Zachariah scoffed out loud. Tristan gave the huntsman a look.

"Oh, come! Surely you have traveled in your life; wandered through many footpaths!"

"None as dangerous as this…"

"Time is wasting. We need to leave now," Tristan ordered, not looking back as he started the walk.

The footpath was well hidden in the mountains, curving around the rocky foundation. If you knew the trail well, you could maneuver through with almost little difficulty. If you were someone who had never set foot in the mountains before, it could be fatal.

Faye, unfortunately, was the latter.

"Don't let go of the side of the mountain," Tristan warned. "It's a long drop."

"Thanks for that," Zachariah grumbled, a hint of sarcasm in his voice. "Tell me again, wise Sorcerer—"

"Wise, *High* Sorcerer!"

Zachariah grumbled again. "*High* Sorcerer…why

can't we fly with a dragon? Or use your 'magic'," he said sarcastically, "to get there?"

"First and foremost," Tristan motioned upwards. Faye and Zachariah followed his gaze and saw the jagged tops of the mountain sides. "This is almost impossible for any creature to maneuver," the High Sorcerer explained. "I have yet to see any creature with wings make it through the mountains; which is why this footpath is perfect."

"You mean terrifying," Faye commented, feeling her face freeze from the blasts of cold wind. The mountain side was rough and cold, but there was a hidden groove that was dug onto the side to help her hold on.

"Second, Kardos put a magic block on the footpath. Ah, here we go," Tristan commented, "one more turn, and…" Tristan gestured toward the open ground, safe from the narrow footpath. "We made it. Now, we are about…halfway there."

Faye glanced uneasily at Zachariah. "I'm sorry, did you say…*halfway?*"

The High Sorcerer nodded. Walking past Faye and winking quickly in her direction once again, he looked around at their surroundings, touching large rocks as he passed them. "Here it is!" Tristan exclaimed. Faye observed Tristan as he appeared to walk straight into a large boulder. Her eyes widened as he vanished. A few moments later, he returned. "Things aren't always what they seem. Follow me."

Zachariah and Faye looked at each other in confusion, but followed. Zachariah laughed softly, nodding in what seemed like understanding. Faye, on the other hand, was still confused.

"Look at it from this way," Zachariah instructed, guiding her to the same spot he was standing in and then walked toward the boulder.

"I see it!" she exclaimed. It wasn't that he walked into the large boulder, but there was an illusion. The boulder concealed a secret path made of stone. Zachariah turned to the young girl, shrugging his shoulders.

"It's not magic, but it's rather impressive," he admitted curtly. Faye giggled softly as she followed behind.

CHAPTER TEN: THE WARNING

AT LAST THEY HAD ARRIVED. After Faye walked through the end of the secret passage, she turned around and now saw a stone wall concealing their entry point. She was about to follow Tristan and Zachariah, but froze in place. On either side of the hall were red and gold patterned tapestries, statues of knights standing on either side of the hallway and torches hanging on the walls.

This was in her dream. Everything suddenly made sense; the King she saw was of Salzar. Faye didn't want to go any farther for fear of seeing the black silk that covered the King's bed from her dream.

"Faye, let's go," Zachariah called to her. She swallowed hard and reluctantly followed. She kept her eyes down and tried not to look at the red and gold tapestries hanging everywhere, but she couldn't help herself. Everywhere Faye looked, there was something red and gold. When they finally made it to a set of large wooden double doors, Tristan knocked three times and waited. When the door opened, it revealed Kardos in his ceremonial garments, his facial expression blank. From behind him stood someone that Faye recognized instantly: the exhausted King Leonus. His brown and gray speckled hair looked softer than in her dream, but there he was, coughing into a silk handkerchief. Tristan and Zachariah bowed instantly.

"Your Highness," the men greeted at the same time.

Faye couldn't feel her legs anymore. "You're alive..." Without warning, she fainted.

***

When Faye opened her eyes, she was in the forest of Janulai.

Sitting up quickly and ignoring the faint dizzy spell she experienced, she gazed around in confusion at the scene; Towering above her was the Grandfather Tree, the grass was as green as she left it...or thought she did.

Zachariah and Tristan were nowhere to be seen, and neither was Rinji.

"Was it all a dream? A crazy, unexplainable yet...amazingly realistic...dream?" she thought to herself as she stood up. She heard thunder rumbling above her, and knew she had to get home as soon as possible. As soon as she stepped out of the forest, the thunder grumbled again, only this time it was louder than the last. Faye looked up to the skies and froze. These weren't normal storm clouds; they were a dark mass of purple and black.

Terrified, Faye ran. She only made it a few feet until a mass of smoke crashed to the ground in front of her, making Faye skid to a halt.

"Surprised?" a voice challenged. Faye continued to stare at the smoky mass. Emerging from the smoke was the woman from her dreams, only she had soft gray eyes. "I've been searching for you, Dragon Whisperer."

Faye's eyes widened. "You-You must have the wrong—I'm no—"

"Silence," the woman ordered casually. "You are a horrible liar." Her gray eyes scanned the area, and then stared back at Faye. "So young to be the chosen one. Marcus was a fool to think he could hide you from me," she snarled, her small mouth forming a scowl.

"How do you know Marcus? What have you done

with him?!" Faye asked, anger and fear stirring in her heart. Black and purple smoke gathered around the stranger until she vanished, her soft yet malicious chuckle growing softer. Faye looked around the empty field, her heart beating hard against her chest. Chills suddenly ran down her spine as the back of her neck grew very cold. She heard a deep inhale from behind her.

"He's *dead*," the woman hissed in her ear.

Faye's blood began to boil. She wouldn't believe he was dead; he couldn't be! Enraged, Faye whirled around and blasted the stranger with a large energy ball that struck the woman to the ground. "He's not dead! LIAR!" she yelled, blasting more energy balls at the woman's direction.

"Such anger for someone so small," the woman teased, her eyes suddenly glowing the same eerie amethyst color from her dream. The energy balls froze in mid air. With a flick of the witch's wrists, they flung back to Faye, who dodged them at the last minute and fell to the ground.

"Hear me, Dragon Whisperer," the woman hissed as a storm of smoke surrounded the two, "I will end your life, but not before I torment you to the point of you begging for the deed to be done," she hissed. The clouds continued to grow, leaving little light for Faye to see the amethyst eyes.

"I demand to know a name!" Faye yelled. "Who are you?"

A high cackle rang through the air as the last of the light was extinguished. The area surrounding Faye became very cold, and from areas unknown, a frigid, harsh wind began to blow. She closed her eyes for a moment, and suddenly saw a ray of light shining down on a body lying on the ground. She cautiously stepped closer to the body until she recognized Marcus' face. It read the same exhausted, tired look as King Leonus had in her dream.

Her knees felt weak as she collapsed to the floor. Tears poured down her cheeks as she cried on his still chest, hoping her tears would wake him from some kind of curse. Suddenly, somewhere in the darkness, Faye heard a roar.

"*Faye,*" Rinji's voice called, "*wake up! Open your eyes! The pain your mind is going through...it's too much for you to handle alone...open your eyes!*"

"Rinji," she whispered softly. "I'm so scared."

"*You have to believe that he isn't gone...it's just a trick the witch set on your mind! Please open your eyes!*"

When Faye opened her eyes, she was staring at a vaulted ceiling. As she sat up slowly and ignored the brief feeling of dizziness, she finally saw Kardos sitting across from her.

"That was quite the greeting to give to His Highness," Kardos commented, handing her a bronze cup full of liquid. "Drink," he ordered. "It will help with the nightmares."

Faye blushed slightly as she took the cup from Kardos. She inspected the contents, smelling the aroma that rose from the liquid. "Vanilla...honey...and berries," she observed. "The 'Shades of Dream' potion?"

Kardos nodded. "You *do* know your potions," he complimented.

She shrugged her shoulders. "It's one of the simpler potions to make. Anyone with a sense of—" she stopped herself from finishing and cleared her throat. "Erm, I mean, thank you." She took a sip to show her gratitude. The warm honey ran down her throat and felt soothing to drink. Soon, she took another sip, more than the first. "What happened?" she asked.

"I could ask you the same thing, Faye," Kardos answered in a cordial manner. Faye looked around the room; red and gold tapestries were shown here, as well as a portrait. It showed the King when he had fewer gray hairs, and a little girl by his side. She had her dark brown hair tied up in a formal manner, and dark brown eyes to match, so big and most likely, Faye imagined, filled with curiosity. "I asked everyone to leave, though it was hard making Tristan follow orders," Kardos grumbled. Faye glanced up at Kardos, shocked at what he said. "Your Elf friend Zachariah of course wanted to stay, but seemed," Kardos hesitated, as if trying to find the right word to use, "apprehensive around the King and myself."

Faye blinked a few times, then smirked. Zachariah was known to be the silent one around others, including ones that know magic. "It was nothing," she lied. "I just got dizzy and—"

"'You're alive.' I believe that's what you said to the King," Kardos recalled aloud. "Now, why would you say something like that? And this time, don't lie."

Faye fiddled with a bit of her green robe in nervousness. "So I *did* say that aloud," she mumbled. Looking up at Kardos with guilty eyes, she sighed. "How has his health been?"

Kardos blinked a few times. "Fine. The King is in good health, high spirits—"

"You don't want me to lie," she confronted the High Sorcerer. "I would appreciate having the same courtesy."

It was Kardos' turn to sigh. "He is unwell. No medicine, nor magic for that matter, has been able to aide him. It's likely he won't be with us much longer." His voice was full of melancholy. "Somehow I have a feeling you already knew."

Faye looked down at her fingers as she fiddled with her fingernails. "There was a dream. About a King." she confessed. "One surrounded in," she took a small gulp and hesitated, "red and gold."

If Kardos was surprised, Faye could not see it. His face was expressionless. "Continue."

Faye nodded. "He was coughing a lot. His kerchief turned red," she finally saw the flash of concern in his eyes and immediately felt guilty for even saying anything. "That-that's all I remember," she lied. Kardos nodded in understanding, but his expression remained solid.

"*Continue*," he ordered softly, raising an eyebrow. The young girl blushed slightly and mentally demerited herself for being a terrible liar.

"You were there with him," she sighed, looking down at her fingernails. "You both were discussing the wedding of his daughter, and you didn't seem interested

116

in the match," she glanced up at him to see a small smirk, but didn't say anything. "The King continued to cough more and more, and I couldn't take it. So, I went out of that room, but…" she couldn't stop the tears from running down her cheeks. Her lip quivered slightly, but she still continued. "The room…the next room was black. Everything. Black silk covered all the walls…and the bed…and he…the King…" She didn't want to utter the words. She didn't want to redescribe the still and unpeaceful body that belonged to the King. She reimagined the discomforted face of King Leonus, alone in the cold room that was draped in black silk. *"Wait,"* she thought to herself, *"he wasn't alone."* Looking back up at Kardos, she blurted, "He wasn't alone. Besides you being there in the beginning, I mean."

Kardos suddenly looked very worried. "Who else was with him?"

Faye shrugged her shoulders. "A—a woman. I have never seen her before, but she knew I was a Dragon Whisperer. She had long black hair, but her eyes…they weren't normal…they were glowing, like…like—"

Kardos grabbed Faye's shoulder, and she felt panic rising in her blood. "Amethysts?" he finished her sentence.

Faye nodded slowly. "How did you know that?" She glanced down at his fists and saw they were clenched so hard, his knuckles were turning white. Kardos let out a frustrated sigh.

"It's Milla, the Sorceress of Baroody," he answered. Then he looked into Faye's eyes. "You're not a child anymore. You deserve to know the truth. What has Tristan told you about her?"

Faye shrugged her shoulders. "You're the only one that knows this. I—I wanted to tell Marcus this, but—well, you know."

Kardos nodded understandingly. "Milla was once a High Sorceress. That is, until she fell in love." He waved his hand in the open air until silver smoke appeared and showed an image of the same woman that haunted her dreams. Rather than looking demonic with her glowing eyes, she seemed happy and peaceful, her gray eyes gazing toward the skies. "She fell in love with a greedy man; a man thirsty for power...King Jedrek." The picture changed to a man with ghost white hair that seemed to contrast the stubble on his black beard. His eyes were a piercing green that Faye had never seen, and hoped she never would. King Jedrek was pacing, combing his fingers through his hair.

"Although she will never admit it, it was the wickedness of the King that changed her," Kardos sighed. Faye could tell he had been thinking about this for a while. "She would do anything for him...kill anyone for him—"

Kardos sighed and hesitated before speaking. "You have to listen to me, Faye. Do not look for your uncle, under any circumstances," he ordered. Faye stared at him in shock. "Milla is not to be underestimated. Her power lies within a demonic place; a place that torments the mind and burns your soul...It has many names, but here it is called the Shadow Realm." Faye suddenly felt sick. Kardos must have noticed, because his worried look multiplied. "You've heard of this?" he asked.

"Just today, in Janulai," Faye responded, still registering the order to not look for Marcus, "we were...attacked. They called themselves the Shadow Realm, and they knew everything about me." Faye recalled the purple and black fire that caught her leg and burned into her skin. She rubbed her leg in response. "They all had amethyst eyes. They had this fire..." she choked on her tears once again. "It was the same kind of fire that killed my p-parents," Without warning, tears flowed down her cheeks. She quickly wiped them away, eyeing Kardos as he waited patiently.

"They aren't *called* Shadow Realm," he informed her softly. "They are called the *Varjo*. They are shadow assassins, controlled by Milla's thoughts. You can not kill them until you've killed her. They are most likely the ones that were responsible for the fire that claimed your parents' lives," he paused for a moment until Faye looked up at him. His eyes were full of sympathy and wisdom. "Something *you* had no control over. It wasn't your fault. Now you must promise me that you will not look for Marcus anymore. It's not safe for you."

"I have to find him! He's like family," she defended.

"He doesn't *want* you to find him!" he hissed in impatience. Faye's eyes widened. If her heart could break anymore, it would have at that moment. Why wouldn't Marcus want her to find him? "One day, you will understand. One day, all the clouds of confusion will be lifted, and things will become clear. Until that day, I ask you not just as High Sorcerer of Salzar, but as a friend," his voice was calm and assuring. "Please don't look for him, Faye."

Faye nodded, but she wasn't satisfied. Why wouldn't he want her to look for him? Was he embarrassed? Ashamed? Was it the progress or lack thereof when it came to her studies? She knew her magic; she thought she was doing well.

"Now," Kardos continued, "Tristan informed me of your newest companion. What is your dragon's name?"

"Rinji," Faye replied, gazing out the large window.

Salzar seemed to be covered in snow, but not a lot. The mountains looked serene, and already Faye began feeling a little relaxed, given the information she just received. "Do you meditate? It's so peaceful up here," she asked, changing the subject.

"Yes," he answered bluntly. "Rinji? How did you come up with that name?" Kardos asked curiously.

"I didn't come up with the name," she explained, confused by the question. "He told me."

"Who told you?" Kardos asked as he touched her shoulder. She glanced behind her and saw the confusion etched on the High Sorcerer's brow.

"*What is so confusing about this?*" she thought to herself. "My...My dragon did. He told me his name is Rinji. Well, he didn't speak, but more...thought it to me? I know it doesn't make any sense, but—"

"What spell?" Kardos asked.

Faye raised an eyebrow. "I'm sorry, I don't understand." She faintly heard the doors open, and the sound of footsteps getting louder.

"What spell did you use to communicate with your dragon? Did Tristan teach you his spell? Or maybe Marcus?" Kardos' tone was more insistent this time.

Faye shook her head. "No, sir. There was no spell. Wait, don't all dragons talk to their Dragon

Whisperers?" she asked. Judging by the look on Kardos'
face, she knew the answer. "No?"

"You can talk to your dragon?" a voice questioned.
Faye looked past Kardos and saw Tristan, who had an
equally surprised expression on his face as Kardos did.
"Without a spell?!"

Faye glanced at the two High Sorcerers nervously.
"Well..."

Tristan crossed his arms and raised an eyebrow.
"What?"

Faye fiddled with her robe once more before gazing
up at Tristan and Kardos, both giving Faye their undi-
vided attention. "It-it's not just Rinji I can understand.
M-Miath—the baker's dragon and Nuria...I've heard
them. Isn't that...you know...something *all* Dragon
Whisperers can do?"

Kardos shook his head silently. "I have never..." his
voice trailed off. "Tristan, you—"

Tristan shook his head, eyeing the young Sorceress.
"No," he said simply.

Kardos paced the room for a little while, mumbling
to himself before facing Faye once more. "Listen to me,
Faye. This gift you have, this power to speak to your
dragon—to dragons in general, is not...normal...for a
Dragon Whisperer."

"This is something Jedrek would surely come after," Tristan added. Faye had forgotten about the Eastern King; the reason Dragon Whisperers were hiding in the shadows and why so many people feared going out at night.

"You can not tell *anyone* about this gift. If Jedrek could have a Dragon Whisperer that could actually...*communicate*...with a dragon," Kardos looked back at Faye, which sent a chill down her spine. She didn't want to find out the rest of that sentence.

"Wait," Faye changed the subject, "Where's...where's Zachariah?" Not receiving any response from Tristan, she hurried outside and looked for her friend. *"He doesn't know his way around the palace."*

"Neither do you," Rinji's voice commented in her mind. *"Don't get lost. He's outside."*

"How do you know that?" she thought.

"I'm here with him, that's how. Much to the female's disapproval," he answered, sounding proud in his accomplishments. *"She wanted me to just wait while...while I could feel your nightmare. I couldn't take being away from you, all the while knowing you were in pain, little one,"* his voice was filled with worry.

"You can feel my...dreams?" she asked, stopping in her tracks.

"Faye," Rinji's voice sounded insistent, and Faye felt a sudden urge of impatience course through her mind. *"We...are...connected. In every way; every thought, every dream, every feeling one feels, so will the other. Now get outside. NOW. There's someone else here too."*

"Who?"

"A woman with long black hair, and I don't like the way she is looking at me." As soon as the thought crossed her mind, she heard a roar come from outside, and felt a strong protective urge.

Faye stopped in the corridor. *"It can't be..."* she thought in fear. *"Rinji, protect Zachariah!"*

"Faye!" a voice called out. She turned around and saw Tristan running towards her.

"It's Milla! She's outside!" Faye gasped. In that moment, Tristan's eyes seemed to change from worried to enraged. His hands glowed a violent, fiery red as he ran outside. Faye followed as fast as she could, worried for the safety of the huntsman and her dragon.

CHAPTER ELEVEN: THE MARK

DIE, DRAGON!" The woman donning a black robe lunged at Rinji, a long blade in her hands. Zachariah continued to counterattack every move the woman made, missing her by mere inches with each strike of his twin daggers. Rinji bared his teeth as the woman and huntsman did their dance.

"Zachariah!" Faye called out in worry. She was about to run over and help, but was stopped by Tristan.

"Wait a moment," he said, his hands not glowing anymore. "This is rather interesting."

"Out of my way, Elf!" the woman hissed. "I didn't think Elves enjoyed the company of dragons," she lunged at him again, the two partaking in a weaponized waltz. Zachariah was able to block another move and shoved the girl away.

"He's a friend," he commented, "and I defend all

friends." Before he could attack again he was blasted by a fireball and fell to the ground. The woman looked to the source of the magic, as did Faye. Tristan smirked, his hands glowing once again.

"I had him, you know," the stranger huffed.

Tristan smirked at the woman, ignoring her pout. "Of course you did, your Highness," he replied with a bow.

Faye raised an eyebrow at Tristan. "'Your Highness?'" she repeated.

Tristan smiled at the young Sorceress. "Faye Haybear, may I present Princess Daralis, daughter of the King of Salzar?" he presented the young woman as she concealed her long blade once more. She tied her long, raven colored hair into a bun, appearing more formal. The Princess was a little taller than Faye, her tan skin bringing out her chocolate colored eyes. "Princess Dara, this is Faye Haybear of Janulai. Faye is training to be a High Sorceress...among other things," he nodded towards Rinji. He then glanced at the huntsman. "Oh, and this is Zachariah, the Elf huntsman," he added in a less-than-interested tone.

Zachariah started to hesitate. Faye had never seen him like this before. He immediately went on bended knee without looking up. "Your Highness, please accept my apologies. I hope I brought no harm upon you."

Princess Dara walked toward the huntsman and stood over him a few moments, waiting. Faye had no idea what she was doing. Then, she used her fingertips to raise the huntsman's head, so he was looking at her. "If only my bodyguards had your..." she paused for a moment, then grazed her hand against his silk scarf, "ambition." They stared at each other for a few more moments until Faye broke the silence.

"Why did you try to attack Rinji?" she asked. *"Are you hurt, Rinji?"* she thought to her dragon.

"No child," he replied, *"your huntsman friend was very good at blocking her every move. You have some talented friends in your life,"* he complimented.

"How did he get here?" Tristan whispered in awe, staring at Rinji. He studied the green dragon, walking around him "I've...I've never...not even Nuria!"

Rinji growled softly. *"That female is too scared. You should be too, High Sorcerer,"* Rinji bared his teeth at Tristan in warning.

"Go easy on him, Rinji. He...he's nice," Faye thought to herself.

Rinji glanced over at Faye and snorted softly. *"You seem to favor him a lot, child."*

Faye could feel the heat rising in her cheeks as

Tristan walked away from the dragon. "How did he maneuver through the mountains?" Tristan asked aloud.

"Forest dragons are experts in being one with the Earth," Rinji explained. *"We know better than anyone how to navigate the terrain with ease."*

"He says being a forest dragon, he can maneuver around the—"

"Faye," Tristan shot her a look of curiosity. "I've only seen dragons of the Air come close to the Mountains...if he's an Earth dragon, he shouldn't—"

"Well, my dragon is special." Faye defended, giving a small smirk to Tristan. Suddenly, she felt a small whack on her arm. She rubbed the area and turned to see Rinji's tail curl away.

"Stop calling me dragon," Rinji growled. Faye could sense impatience coursing through her again.

"Okay, okay...sorry...*Rinji* is special." Faye rolled her eyes at the large green dragon, feeling a sense of pride once more. *"Happy?"*

"Yes. Quite so."

The Princess raised an eyebrow. "Who is she...?" She glanced at Tristan, who only pointed at the dragon. "Oh. This is...oh my!" Now the Princess of Salzar bowed before Faye. "Forgive me Dragon Whisperer! I thought it was one of *Jedrek's*..."

128

Faye's eyes widened in surprise. "Please! Please Princess, no! Don't do that...g-get off the ground." she begged, her cheeks heating up. Zachariah rose from the ground and assisted the beautiful Princess to her feet. "How did you know I was—"

"Stories were told that all the dragons and Dragon Whisperers were in Jedrek's power; all of them Shadowed—possessed by a power that came from the Shadow Realm. To think, I would have..." she looked down at her hand holding Zachariah's hand. "So soft," she admired, suddenly changing the subject. Princess Dara continued to stare at his hand until someone cleared their throat loudly. They all turned to see Kardos standing behind Faye, his eyes never leaving the Princess and huntsman.

"Princess," Kardos bowed, "your father is expecting you." Faye watched the Princess' expression transform from curious to melancholy in that one moment.

"Very well," she sighed sadly. "Probably to talk about my future punishment," she mumbled, misery dripping from her voice. She glanced at Faye and subtly nodded her head. "Dragon Whisperer, I hope our paths cross again one day." She then turned to Zachariah and smiled. "Thank you for the entertainment. I enjoyed fighting you," she teased.

"Perhaps we will fight together next time, Princess," the huntsman bowed respectfully. Grabbing a kerchief from the inside of her sleeve, she placed it in his hand, giving a noticeable squeeze.

"Until that day, huntsman," she nodded, turning around and heading for the castle.

"If what you were saying is true, Faye," Kardos commented, "you should warn the Kings of Janulai and Arana. I will do my part here and inform the King on Milla. Now that you have your Mark, be careful. The *Varjo* will stop at nothing until they find you. Tristan, you know what to do. Take some horses. The less obvious you seem to be, the better." Without saying another word, he turned on his heel and left, the guards closing the gates behind him.

When Faye turned around, she saw the sky turning different colors as the sun began to set. How long were they inside for?!

"Well," Tristan sighed, "there is no way we are traveling overnight. Let's go into town and get some food, horses, and rest. Faye, Rinji has to go into hiding. Nuria will show him a good place to rest. When we leave the town, 'channel' your way to Rinji's mind," he used hand signals as he instructed the young girl. "Nuria will show him how to get to Arana in the morning." He motioned for Faye and Zachariah to follow him. "For now, we walk on foot."

"Wait!" a voice called out. The three travelers turned around to see a maid running towards them. She was so short, one could have mistaken her for a child if it wasn't for the gray accenting her coal-black hair that was kept in a tight bun. "The Princess is rather insistent on the three of you staying the night. No need to be wandering around these woods at night, with the Kay-Tahs lurking about and all."

Faye raised an eyebrow. "The-the what?"

The maid shuddered. "The Kay-Tahs. Nasty little troll-like beings with grubby hands that like to grab things that aren't theirs. I had a run in with them once," she shook her head. "Won't be happening again anytime soon! Now, come on. She'll not take 'no' for an answer," the maid insisted, ushering the three inside the palace. Faye turned back towards Rinji.

"I'll be right here," Rinji's voice echoed in her mind as the palace doors began to close.

"I'll be takin' care of you, miss," the maid announced. "Arrielle's the name, miss. The two of you will have someone caring for you as well." As she explained that, two male servants rounded the corner, leading Zachariah and Tristan to their separate rooms.

"Now, let's get you out of these clothes and into something more comfortable," she instructed.

As they headed down another corridor, Arrielle was barking orders at younger servants. "I'm the 'Lady of the Maids', they call me," she chuckled loudly. "Should be called 'Lady of the Gossipers.' Mother hen for all these little ones. Make sure they—HEY! I need fresh linen for our guest here. HOP TO IT!" she barked at two servant girls gossiping. Faye smirked as she pictured Arrielle as Little Verna back in Janulai, and wondered who was actually louder. She continued to follow Arrielle until she suddenly stopped and opened a door.

"This will be your room for the night," she informed Faye. The young Sorceress couldn't believe the spacious guest room she was given. The bed was twice as large as her own, with at least five goose feather pillows covering the top. The bed frame had beautiful red silk fabric draping over the top as if it was a canopy. The walls were a beautiful bronze color that made the red silk look like a warm ember.

"Wow," Faye gasped softly.

"I know," Arrielle sighed, "it *is* rather small." Faye looked over at the maid in shock, only to receive loud, barking laughter in response. "I'm only joking! Come now, let's get you out of these dirty things. We will have a bath drawn for you momentarily."

A bath!? Faye smiled to herself. After a while, a few servant girls poured buckets of hot water into an empty tub, finishing the touch with rose petals and left. Faye relaxed, scrubbing the dirt and grime off her fingernails and everywhere else she could get clean, and then closed her eyes, enjoying the aroma of roses. After a while, she looked at her hands and noticed they were pruning. The water was losing its warmth as well.

As if on cue, Arrielle and another younger maid entered the room with towels. "Right then," Arrielle sighed, "Out you get! Got some warm towels for you to dry with." She opened the towel and motioned for Faye to stand up. As she did, the younger maid screamed.

"What is that?! Witchcraft!" she yelled, running out of the room in terror. Faye looked around in distress, suddenly realizing her Mark was visible. It had also crossed her mind that she hadn't even seen her own Mark yet.

"I am so sorry for that, miss!" Arrielle shook her head. "She'll be getting lashes for that outburst!"

"NO! No no, that's alright..." Faye shook her head, wrapping a towel around herself. "I just—I need a looking glass, that's all. Two, if possible." Arrielle hurried out, but Faye could hear her yelling at the maid.

A few moments later, she returned, two small mirrors in hand.

"Here you go, miss." she said with a smile, but Faye could hear the nervousness in her voice.

"Can you hold one of the mirrors behind me? I'd like to—" before Faye could finish, Arrielle handed her one of the mirrors and hurried behind her. Faye took a deep breath and held the mirror up until she could see Arrielle and the reflection of her back.

If Faye were that younger maid, she would have screamed too. Her left hand trembled as she grazed her fingertips over the shimmering green and yellow scales that were now melded with her skin. The scales had the same color and texture as Rinji's, and covered most of her back. "The Mark isn't just a Mark," she gasped, still staring in awe at the new patch of skin she had. "It's the scales of a dragon...*my* dragon. *That's* the Mark of the Dragon Whisperer."

CHAPTER TWELVE: THE TREATY

FAYE COULDN'T SLEEP. She tossed and turned in her oversized bed, willing herself to sleep but failing miserably. She had never slept anywhere this extravagant. Groaning in frustration, she crawled out of bed and put on the silk slippers and robe that were already prepared for her. She opened the door slowly and tiptoed out of the room.

Even though it was night, there were still workers cleaning floors and completing their usual tasks. One maid hesitated before running out of the hallway, leaving her scrubbing brush behind. She had a feeling word had gotten out about her Mark. It was like Arrielle hinted; these ladies were gossipers.

"That's her...the woman with the Mark..."

"I heard she was born with it...:"

"...such a curse..."

Faye stopped and glared at the three women speaking in loud whispers. The glare seemed to have silenced them as they hurriedly continued their work. Faye eventually found her way back outside to discover Rinji curled up not too far from the palace doors. As she walked silently towards the dragon, she felt a hint of tension course through her body.

"You really should never sneak up on a dragon, little one," Rinji's thoughts sounded slightly amused.

Faye stopped in her tracks. "I'm going to need to get used to that," she whispered. Rinji lifted his head and looked directly at Faye, growling softly. She suddenly felt slightly worried for some reason.

"Is that what humans wear for sleeping?" Rinji asked curiously. *"It's no wonder your kind get ill at night!"* Faye wasn't even thinking about the cold, but suddenly a shiver trailed up her spine. Was it because of the strange connection she had with Rinji, or was it truly the cold?

"I'll be right back," she stated as she hurried back inside the palace. She sprinted through the hallways until she found her room once more. Grabbing a few unused logs that rested by the fireplace, she carefully headed back towards the outer doors. As she rounded a corner, she stopped in her tracks and hid by the wall. Peering around the corner, she spotted Princess Dara wandering by a doorway, seeming almost hesitant about something. When she was sure she wasn't paying attention, Faye darted past, and slipped out the door, being welcomed by the crisp night air once again.

"*Clever girl,*" Rinji stated. She felt a sense of pride flush over her.

"*I'm really going to need to get used to this,*" she thought to herself as she placed the logs down on the ground and took a few steps back. The young Sorceress watched as Rinji's chest slowly began to glow a soft orange color. The color began to rise from his chest, to his neck, until he opened his mouth and a small fireball emitted from his mouth and struck the logs. A fire immediately came to life as Faye sat near Rinji. "I couldn't sleep," she mumbled. She traced her fingers across Rinji's scales as she recalled the events that happened; it all felt like a dream as the memories blurred together in her mind.

"*Calm your thoughts, little one,*" Rinji's thoughts echoed in her mind. "*Who is this Marcus that you're always thinking about? He's in most of your thoughts.*"

Faye's heart sank a little when she heard his name. "He-he practically raised me. He was friends with my parents—they died when I was younger," she explained out loud. "I—I tried to save them. I didn't care about myself, I—I just wanted my mom and dad." Faye pushed up the silk sleeve from her robe and gazed at her scars. "I-I got burned from the fire. Marcus pulled me away...he saved me," she recalled the memory as she traced her fingers along her forearm.

"*He means a lot to you,*" Rinji's voice was soft and low as he sniffed at the scars on her arm.

"Rinji—"

"*Use your thoughts, little one,*" Rinji suggested. "*You never know if you're truly alone or not.*" The warning caused Faye to shudder. "*Don't be afraid,*" Rinji nudged her shoulder, "*right now, we are alone. I only want you to practice,*" he assured her.

"Wh—okay," she hesitated. "*You said you saw me when I was in the forest—by the Grandfather Tree,*" Faye pictured the Grandfather Tree in her mind. "*Wh—well, why didn't you visit me then? Why did you wait?*"

There was silence for a few moments. Rinji raised his head up and looked up at the sky. "*You weren't ready,*" he answered simply, "*but that wasn't the only time I saw you.*"

"*It wasn't?*"

"*No, little one. I've been watching you since you got lost in the woods...it was raining and you didn't know where you were going..."* Faye's cheeks became red. So many questions rushed through her mind, but Rinji only paid attention to one. *"I didn't show myself then, because the huntsman was already there. You had so much going through your mind and heart, little one...adding a dragon to your conscience would be more troublesome to you than needed."*

"I don't understand," Faye thought to herself. *"When I got lost...that was before I was told about—"*

"Your Mark, yes...but I knew...I knew you and I were destined to be together."

"How?"

"...I do not know, little one. I...I just knew."

Faye blinked in confusion, then sighed and looked down at her hands. *"So,"* she finally thought, *"What happens if I die? Or...if you...?"*

"Will you die if I die?" Faye suddenly felt a pang of sadness as she glanced up at Rinji and his moment of silence. *"Yes, child. Just like our emotions, our souls...our very lives are intertwined now. We are one."*

"I see," Faye thought to herself. The young Sorceress began playing with her silk robe as she prayed silently that she wouldn't be responsible for the death of this creature.

"Faye," Rinji's voice echoed in her mind again. *"I*

know we can figure this out together. You just need to believe in yourself. You are destined for wonderful and amazing things. The only person in your way of that...is you."

Feeling a sense of hope, she curled up slightly by Rinji and began to close her eyes, listening to the slow, rhythmic breathing of her new friend and companion.

***

Faye slowly opened her eyes and observed the burned logs, the embers barely glowing inside. Rinji's large body was curled behind her, his tail being used as a place to rest her head. She smiled as she heard him snore softly. Slowly, she got up and quietly left her resting spot.

"Faye?"

Faye smirked and shook her head, knowing in the back of her mind Rinji would have been aware. *"I'm fine, Rinji. Go back to sleep,"* she assured him. Within a few moments, soft snoring was heard from the dragon once more. Faye smiled to herself as she headed back inside the palace. As she continued walking down the corridors, tracing her fingers along the fabric of the tapestries, she heard muffled coughing. Curious, Faye leaned in closer to the door. Suddenly, the door opened towards her, causing the door to hit the side of her head. Leaving the room was Kardos, who didn't look too happy to see Faye.

"You should be in bed," he insisted.

"Is that the Dragon Whisperer?" a weak voice called out. Faye peered past the High Sorcerer and saw King Leonus; his expression appeared tiresome, yet his eyes showed a sparkle as he motioned the young girl forward. She glanced uneasily towards Kardos, who stepped aside and nodded in the direction of the King.

"Remember who you're talking to," Kardos reminded her in whisper as she proceeded inside the room. When the door shut, she curtsied in an awkward manner.

"Y-Your Majesty," she greeted. The King nodded to her and motioned her towards his bed. She looked around and saw there were no longer red and gold silks, but black. She could feel her heart beating hard against her chest with each step she took. She held back her tears as she saw King Leonus' eyes and the sparkle inside them. The rest of his face appeared tired; his brow was furrowed with restlessness, yet his eyes still sparkled. Faye thought that maybe it was the last glimmer of hope that shone in his eyes.

"I know I am dying," he wheezed, nodding his head

slowly. "I do not fear it anymore. In fact, I welcome it with open arms." The King attempted to extend his arms, but they barely moved.

Faye stared at the King in shock. "Y-Your Majesty, perhaps your daughter...?"

He slowly shook his head. "I have already said my goodbyes to her," he confessed. "Sit down, Faye," he commanded. Faye did as he ordered. "I always believed in the word of a gentleman. When I was a much younger King, my wife was still walking on the Earth, and my daughter was just a toddler, I signed a peace treaty with the King of Baroody. At the time," he hesitated as he took a slow breath, "it was Jedrek's father, Killian. Grab that parchment, there," he motioned behind Faye. She turned around and retrieved the envelope. It was sealed with red wax with the emblem of the mountains of Starrain. "That is the true copy of the treaty. We each have one, each sealed with red wax bearing our crest. The treaty said that we were to be united through marriage.

"My daughter, Daralis, was going to be joined in matrimony to Killian's eldest son, Prince Isaac. In the event of war being declared by either of us upon the other, the treaty would be broken. King Jedrek," he coughed a little, "he broke that treaty two years ago, yet feels he is still entitled to marry my daughter." Faye remained silent, listening to every word. "Jedrek was always a selfish boy, but Dara and Isaac, they got along wonderfully." A small smile formed on his lips.

"One night, a delivery man appeared with what looked to be the treaty King Killian had signed. Something inside me told me it was a lie. The wax bared Killian's crest, yet it was black as coal. I have always been a peaceful man," he confessed, "so I never said anything to avoid a war. I now know I was a fool." Tears filled in the King's eyes as he continued. "My daughter will now be betrothed to him in two night's time, and I will be joining my wife soon, unable to protect my precious daughter from the evil outside the palace walls. You must promise me," he held onto Faye's hand, "that you will bring the treaty to the other Kings, informing them that the treaty is broken, and beg for them to protect my daughter. Arana is known for their weaponry, Janulai—well, you know they are known for their crops, medicines..and you." He squeezed her hand, which unfortunately was barely a grip to begin with. "Promise me," his breathing became faster and heavier, "Promise me you-you will take care of m-my daughter. Please," he begged.

"I—I promise," she said, doubt haunting the back of

her mind. King Leonus gave a reassuring nod and released his hold on Faye. She didn't know what else to say. What could she do that armies couldn't?! She had just received her Mark, met her dragon, and ran from the Shadow Realm all in one day. Now she had to make a promise to a dying King.

"Don't doubt yourself, Dragon Whisperer," he wheezed once more. "You were destined for wonderful...amazing...things," he uttered. With that, he closed his eyes as he took one last breath.

Faye cried as she let go of the King's lifeless hand. *"How could I make that promise to him?"* she thought to herself. She barely heard the door open as she continued to stare at the King.

"Faye," the voice beckoned. She looked up and saw Kardos standing by the door, a sorrowful expression on his face. He nodded to Faye, and she obediently followed. She remained silent, ignoring the stares from the servant girls, their whispers cold like ice. Kardos led Faye back to her room. "We will talk tomorrow. Get some rest," he suggested.

She stared up into his eyes, her own eyes filled with tears. "How can anyone sleep after something like that?" she yelled. Kardos remained still, not showing any emotion. "First, I get attacked by Shadow Realm—No, what did you call them?? Oh, *Varjo*—get struck by one, meet my dragon, get my Mark—which by the way HURT LIKE HELL!" She yelled once more, taking frantic breaths, "*Then* I get told I can never see Marcus, the man who was practically a father to me, and now I made a promise to a DEAD KING that I can't even keep!" Tears streamed down Faye's reddened cheeks as a door opened. She whirled around to see Zachariah appear out in the hallway in silk pajama pants. Faye stared in shock, never having seen the huntsman without a shirt, let alone without the silk cover that normally concealed the lower portion of his face. His mouth was thin, yet his lips were a pinkish color like the cherry blossoms that bloom in Spring. He had scars that ran along his cheeks, chin, and neck. She would never have known of his unique features with the silk shroud always obscuring so much of his appearance. She could tell he was embarrassed and assumed it was because he felt exposed without his silk.

"Go back to your room, huntsman," Kardos suggested firmly. As he gave the order, Princess Dara emerged from behind Zachariah, wearing a silk robe. The huntsman looked down, not looking at Faye as she glanced from the Princess to her best friend. "Princess," Kardos shook his head, "please tell me you—"

"Yes," she stated firmly, grasping onto Zachariah's hand. "We did."

Faye blinked multiple times and shook her head in shock. Speechless at what she heard and saw, she entered her room and quickly shut the door. Even though she was alone, she could hear the arguments that were shouted in the corridors.

"I don't love him!"

"You are betrothed to—"

"I DON'T CARE ABOUT A STUPID TREATY!"

"Then you have damned us all!"

Faye closed her eyes tight, hiding in bed under her cool blankets. She wanted the day to be over. She wanted things to go back to the way they were. Unfortunately, she knew...deep inside...things would never be the same again.

CHAPTER THIRTEEN: THE WOODEN DAGGER

THE SUN PEEKED THROUGH THE CLOUDY DAY. Faye had finished getting dressed, wearing her green hooded robe that was clean of the dirt that covered it before. When she opened her door and stepped out, the mood of the servants matched the day: gloomy and melancholy.

She moved silently through the halls, hearing some maids cry at the news of the passing King.

"I can't believe he...he..." she heard one whimper.

"All I know is, with no King, Jedrek is going to be coming soon," another maid shook her head in disbelief. "Well, you won't find me here. No, siree! I'll be out of here before nightfall." Similar words were whispered

147

throughout the halls as Faye stepped outside, the crisp, cold air greeting her face. She followed the crowd as they took a snowy path, torches in hand, deeper into the mountains.

"Faye," a voice called out. She turned around to see Zachariah hurry by her side, pardoning himself as he made his way around a few maids and butlers. "I asked around. It seems that the royal family, wanting to keep things in the mountains, built a burial chamber...*in the mountains*. The ceremony lasts three days, so we...we might as well stay."

"Right," Faye sighed, "that being the *only* reason you want to stay here."

Zachariah sighed, nodding his head. "I just want you to know," he whispered, "We—we didn't—the Princess only came into my room last night to talk about her father and the treaty, and—" he was going to say something else, but Faye stopped him by raising a hand up slightly.

"Don't," she stated simply. "What you do in your time is just that...your time. It's just," she fiddled with the strap of her satchel. She wanted to tell him how it was unfair that she had been his friend since she was eight years old, and never had the opportunity to see what was under the silk scarf until by chance last night.

Something the Princess already saw. "...Never mind."

The rest of the walk was silent, until they eventually stopped at a large, wooden gate, elaborately decorated in crystals and gems alongside the wood. Guards surrounded either sides of the wooden gate, standing at attention. Faye and Zachariah made it to the front of the crowd, watching as Kardos, Tristan, and Princess Daralis, all wearing black, stood by the door, a black silk covering something in front of the three. An icy chill ran down Faye's spine as she visualized the forever sleeping body of King Leonus.

"My friends," Kardos' voice echoed through the skies. "Today, we mourn the loss of our King...King Leonus, ruler of Salzar, Lord of the Labrintas Mountains...a loving father...and a most dear friend. He lived a long life, and now is reunited with our beautiful Queen. If he were here, he would tell you...do not be sad. Be strong! A mountain does not cry when the wind tries to move it." Murmurs of agreement was heard throughout the crowd. Faye looked at Zachariah with a puzzled look, never having heard a phrase like that before, but shrugged her thoughts off and glanced back towards the front.

Princess Dara stepped towards the black silk, leaning over her father's still body. She kissed his forehead, and placed a small, wooden dagger in his hands. Tears streamed silently from Princess Dara's face, yet her face showed no emotion. Cries were heard throughout the crowd for those that could not hold back their tears. Faye felt an overwhelming rush of emotion, her heart sinking as the sadness swept over her. Instinctively she held onto Zachariah's hand and gave it a squeeze. Memories of her own parent's funeral flooded her mind, the feeling of loss and abandonment revisiting her. Even though their bodies were ashes after the fire, Faye could still feel their souls.

"She's so strong," Faye whispered. She looked up at Zachariah as tears silently flowed down her cheeks. Zachariah's eyes mirrored an identical sadness as he hugged his crying friend.

A captain barked an incoherent order and the guards, in perfect unison, formed two parallel lines starting at the large wooden gate and finishing close to the King. Kardos' hands began to glow a brilliant blue as he gently touched the covered body. Faye watched in silence as the body lifted in the air, floating slowly towards the wooden doors. Kardos' left hand continued to control the floating body as his right hand pointed towards the wooden gate. The decorative gems around the gate glowed brilliantly as the gate slowly opened.

The covered body, floating over the Princess — whose fingers brushed against the draping blanket — entered the cavern, with Kardos following alone. Everyone stood motionless as they waited for his return. After a few moments, Kardos returned from inside the mountain, his hands glowing a brilliant blue once more as the gems lost their glow and the doors sealed shut. The silent crowd, save for a few soft cries, turned and slowly made their way back to the palace.

***

The palace corridors were silent. Faye sat in her room and gazed out her window, which overlooked the mountains. Just then there was a knock at her door.

"Come in," she called out. The door opened and appearing from the other side was Princess Dara, candle in hand. She looked exhausted; her hair was disheveled, her eyes looked bloodshot and her face blotchy and wet from tears.

"Dragon Whisperer, I—I'm so sorry to bother you," the Princess whispered as she stood by the door. "I just —I—"

"Of course, of course!" Faye leaped out of her seat and ushered the grieving Princess inside and closed the door. "Please, come in!" The Princess sat in the large bed, her legs tucked underneath her as Faye filled two cups with water. "Here, drink this," Faye handed the Princess one of the glasses. With a shaky hand, Dara obliged, nodding silently.

"I—I can't believe he's gone," she sighed after taking a small gulp of water.

"I'm sorry for your loss," Faye looked down at her fingers, not sure if she should look at the Princess or not. "I—I know what it's like to lose family. My parents died when I was seven." Faye looked up and noticed the Princess was already staring at her. Her eyes showed sympathy and understanding.

"My mother, she...she never approved of my passion for swordplay," the Princess chuckled softly. "She always told me 'Daralis, a Princess does not need to meddle with weaponry. Now, fix your dress and practice your dancing.' I always said that swordplay was a type of dance, and one day, my father heard me." Princess Dara tucked some of her hair behind her ear. "He pulled me into his throne room one day, and I thought, 'oh no...I'm going to get in trouble.' I never had been so wrong. Instead of punishing me, he—he made me a small wooden sword, and encouraged me to practice. He said, 'Fighting is a type of dance that you need to study...but don't tell your mother.'" Princess Dara laughed loudly at the memory and Faye couldn't help but laugh along.

"So that's where the wooden dagger came from," Faye thought to herself as the laughter died down.

"Ever since that day, I practiced. I practiced and practiced. My arms were tired—I was just exhausted, and there were times when Kardos trained me harder than I thought possible...until the following day."

Faye's eyes widened. "Kardos taught you?"

The Princess nodded. "He's an amazing teacher; he has more patience than he lets on." Dara looked down at her thumbs, fiddling with her nails. "Now that my father is gone...Jedrek is the ruler of this Kingdom," she shuddered at the thought, then grabbed the young Sorceress' hands. "I can't marry him, Faye!" she cried. "I don't love him...and he certainly doesn't love me."

Faye bit her bottom lip. "Well, technically, you're not married to him yet, Princess," Faye thought out loud. "Doesn't that make *you* ruler of the Kingdom?"

Dara paused for a moment, her eyes suddenly lighting up. "Yes! Yes—oh, Faye! You are absolutely correct! *I'm* the ruler of the Kingdom! There must be something I can do...for my Kingdom...for my people—"

"Where are they, anyway?" Faye asked, then covered

her mouth. "I-I'm sorry, Princess. What I meant was...why did none of the villagers attend the funeral?"

"The villages are deep within the mountains; more labyrinths to uncover one day. The villagers know that once my father dies, Jedrek will come with his army...his people...his demons. His last wish was to buy them enough time for them to flee; not to inform anyone until the third day of his passing. But with me ruling," Dara grinned, "I might be able to change that."

Faye's heart dropped. "Princess? What are you—?"

"Goodnight, Faye! I have much to take care of!" Dara exclaimed, a brilliant smile on her face as she ran out the door.

Faye groaned and collapsed into bed, covering her eyes with her arms. "What did I just do?"

***

Faye waited outside for the others. She had hoped to see the Princess, since the last time she spoke to her was three days ago. When she asked Arielle about her whereabouts, she only laughed.

"Hah! You're just as curious as the rest of the gossipers here," Arielle groaned, "but to answer your question, I haven't seen her since the funeral. HEY!

Those blankets aren't gonna fold themselves!"

The young Sorceress' mind was brought back to the present when Rinji nudged her. She gazed up at her dragon companion.

"I'm sure the Princess is fine, little one," Rinji's voice was full of assurance. Faye nodded silently in agreement. She knew what the Princess was going through, but after their conversation a few days ago, Faye wasn't sure of Princess Dara's emotional state. Her mind was forced back to the present when Rinji nudged the young girl. Faye turned around and watched as Tristan and Zachariah started walking towards them.

"Surely we can just...go back through that—that passageway!" Zachariah objected. "Why must we—"

"Why must we ride through the mountaintops, risking life and limb as we pass the jagged peaks?" Tristan finished the Huntsman's sentence. "Because this is much more interesting," he stated nonchalantly, turning to Faye and her dragon. "Right, then. You two ready?"

"He seems overconfident," Rinji commented snidely. *"I can change that."*

"Don't even think about it," Faye muttered, low enough for the two other passengers not to notice as she climbed up first; Faye sat closest to Rinji's neck to give

155

room for the other two. In an instant, Zachariah sat close behind her, while Tristan sat behind the Huntsman, an unimpressed look on his face. "Rinji, take us close to the villages," she instructed. Without warning, Rinji took to the skies. He spun past a jagged peak, dodging it with great ease as he maneuvered through the narrow openings. Faye felt Zachariah's grip tighten around her waist and saw the Huntsman's eyes shut tight as he cursed softly in Elfish.

"Elves aren't used to flying, it seems," Faye observed her brave friend.

"He will manage," Rinji stated simply as he rose higher past the peaks.

"Remarkable!" Tristan gasped in awe, "I've never...I've never seen anyone—*anything*—"

Rinji let out a satisfied roar that echoed in the skies as he dove down, the ground coming closer. Faye's heart felt as if it was beating out of her chest.

"Rinji!" Faye screamed through the rushing wind, but she stopped screaming as she felt a rush of assurance flow through her, the same feeling Marcus would give her when she was younger and scared at night. Sure enough, The dragon slowed his speed, angling his wings differently as their descent slowed until they landed safely in a field. Tristan slid down Rinji, brushing his hand along the green scales.

"Simply remarkable," he admired once more, ignoring Zachariah's groans of nausea. "From here, we travel by foot."

***

Once they made it to a nearby stable, and after Tristan convinced the owner with a few silver coins, they rode into the woods on two horses; Tristan's horse was gray in color with a long, black mane, while Zachariah and Faye's horse was a simple chestnut brown color. Faye looked up towards the skies, watching Rinji fly ahead, his wings causing the trees to bend. She felt a pang of hunger that wasn't her own and chuckled softly. "Rinji is hungry," she whispered to Zachariah.

He turned her her, eyes wide. "What does he think he is going to eat?!"

"Quiet," Tristan snapped. The horses nickered uneasily as they were forced to stop. Faye and Zachariah's eyes observed their surroundings; all was quiet, save for some wildlife ambiance. Just then, there was a rustling sound coming from behind them. Faye turned around and threw an energy ball towards an

157

anonymous hooded stranger with a black horse.

"Not another step," Faye warned, her voice stern, but the hooded rider continued forward. "One more step and I will *not* miss!" Faye yelled. Just then, the stranger raised their hand, and Faye noticed that it wasn't a man's, but a woman's hand. Her heart skipped a beat as her hands reached for the hood.

No one said a word as Princess Daralis' long, black hair tumbled out of the hood, her chocolate eyes locking onto Faye.

CHAPTER FOURTEEN: THE KAY-TAHS

"YOU HAD TO PROMISE THE KING." Faye sighed as Tristan continued to complain. "You couldn't leave things alone?"

"What was I supposed to do?!" Faye hissed back. "He was *dying*, Tristan...and yes, she technically is Queen without a King, but when I told her that, I didn't know—"

"No, you didn't," Tristan grumbled. "Now we have to be extra careful riding to Arana now."

Faye was about to say something in retaliation when there was the sound of movement somewhere in the area. They were surrounded by many noises: rustling of leaves, snapping of twigs, and birds flying away. Without saying a word, the four got off their horses and armed themselves. Faye glanced over at the

Princess who grabbed a sword from one of the bundles that were tied to the horse and couldn't help but spy a crossbow and hilts from a few other swords peeking out of the cloth.

"Are all those weapons?!" Faye whispered to the Princess.

She nodded without looking at Faye. "More or less. I do have some articles of clothing as well," she whispered. "Who's out there?" The Princess called out. Her voice was unwavering and loud. "Come out! I command you to come out!"

"Oh, the little Princess commands Lor-Lor," a scratchy voice sneered. Out of the shrubbery appeared a small creature. It had moss for hair, a lumpy body covered in fur, and was at the height of Faye's knees. Its teeth were brown and yellow, and its large, bulb-like nose had a small wart also covered in hair.

"What is it?" Faye whispered in disgust. She had never seen anything so hideous in her life. "He looks—"

"I'm a lady!" Lor-Lor spat at the young Sorceress. Faye took a nervous gulp.

"Kay-Tahs," Tristan sighed. "I forgot they were around these woods," he admitted. "Hello, Lor-Lor."

"Well, if it isn't the Doomsdayer!" Lor-Lor snapped. Out of nowhere, more Kay-Tahs arrived, all of them creeping toward Tristan while hissing "Doomsdayer!".

"Seems like they know you," Zachariah observed

"They should," he nodded. "I did this to them."

Faye's eyes went wide. "You—wait a moment. These Kay-Tahs were people?!"

"Yes, Kay-Tahs were people," one Kay-Tah answered. "Happy, we were. Living our lives peacefully," he made a small sniffle as he wiped a large tear away, "Until Doomsdayer arrived and did this to us. To Gil, and Gil's beautiful wife," he motioned to Lor-Lor, which made Faye stifle a cough.

"Oh, don't give them that!" Tristan growled. "You know what you did, Gil!" He pointed at the crying troll. "You stole from people; good, hard working people! They had hearts of gold and would always give to those that needed it. You and your...troop," he scoffed, "they did whatever you told them to do. And Lor-Lor," he shook his head at the female troll. "You had friends. You have a husband that loves you. It was never enough for you," he turned back to Faye. "If Lor-Lor wasn't the center of attention and if she wasn't happy, then no one could be happy. She once—" he chuckled dryly, "she once tried to force someone to leave their kindred spirit and stay with her. When her so called friend refused, Lor-Lor killed them both. Lor-Lor hates being alone.

161

Well, now she can never be alone. The Kay-Tahs can never leave the woods and are banned from Arana."

Faye hesitated before speaking. "Wait...they lived in—"

"Arana. I was only twenty-one when I cast them away and made their insides match their outsides; ugly, cold, and bitter."

"And now you're in the middle of the woods," Lor-Lor sneered. "Miles away from the nearest town. Get the Penalty Stick!" she commanded. Suddenly, one of the Kay-Tahs brought forward something that caught Faye's eye.

Diamonds. Four glimmering diamonds on the Penalty Stick. "Wait," she called out, walking straight towards Lor-Lor, who armed herself in defense.

"G-Get away from Lor-Lor!" she cried.

"That staff," she pointed to the staff. "Where did you get it?"

"This is Lor-Lor's Penalty Stick. No one else's! No Staff! Man gave to Lor-Lor fair!" she cried.

Faye's heart stopped. "I know this piece. It was Marcus' walking staff. He would always travel with it. He shouldn't be too far," she looked to the others, hope still alive in her heart. Marcus was alive. She knew he was. "Give me the staff," she commanded. "I need it."

Lor-Lor's eyes went wide as she screamed. "NO! It's Lor-Lor's! Faye can't have it!"

"You don't understa—wait," Faye hesitated. "How did you know my name?"

Lor-Lor smirked. "Kay-Tahs hear things, Faye. Kay-Tahs saw woman with shiny eyes," she explained, a wild spark in her own eyes. "Made deal with her."

Faye began breathing faster. She glanced over at Tristan, who looked enraged. "What *kind* of deal?" Tristan growled. Some of the Kay-Tahs quivered and began backing away slowly, but Lor-Lor stood her ground.

"Human again. For her," she pointed a grubby finger at Faye. "Easy trade. Lor-Lor gets to be beautiful again and live in Arana once more. All Kay-Tahs will. All this for stupid girl."

"*Rinji, they know who I am.*" Faye thought. Fear took over her mind. She began thinking of how she would die; in the woods by a woman with amethyst eyes. Never to see Marcus again...

"I wouldn't do that if I were you," Zachariah threatened, aiming an arrow at Gil. "Unless you want to see your husband draw his last breath." Gil cowered in fear, looking desperately to his wife.

"Lor-Lor can find another," she shrugged her shoulders. Gil stared at her in shock.

163

"Lor-Lor! Gil loves Lor-Lor!" he begged.

"What do Kay-Tahs have to fear with pointy sticks and weapons? Amethyst Lady will take care of us. Her and the Ruler of all dragons! Gil, go get Faye!"

Gil stared at Faye, hesitant at first. Then a mischievous grin covered his face as he lunged toward her.

"Wait!" Faye cried out. "What about a trade? You— you like trading, yes?" she asked. Lor-Lor tilted her head in interest.

"Lor-Lor like trading, yes. But what could be a better trade than being human?" she challenged. Suddenly, a loud roar echoed in the skies. In a matter of seconds, standing between Faye and the Kay-Tahs was Rinji, who looked beyond enraged. The Kay-Tahs screamed in terror, most of them running away.

"DRAGON!" they cried. "Dragon eats Kay-Tahs!"

"I would never want that taste in my mouth," Rinji's voice echoed in her mind as he let out a menacing growl.

"Well, I will trade you... the staff and free passage through these woods...for your life. I think you would prefer to live, unless I'm mistaken." Faye looked at the cowering trolls as they stared up in awe at the majestic green dragon. "My dragon will never harm you nor your family if you agree. However," Faye warned, "if there is any sign of treachery or deceit, the deal is off and he will take your lives."

Lor-Lor stared hesitantly at Rinji as smoke trailed out of his nostrils. She threw the stick to Faye. "Deal. Now, go away! Tell the dragon to leave!" she cried. With that, the Kay-Tahs ran back into the woods for safety.

"Do dragons really eat Kay-Tahs?" Princess Dara asked after a few passing moments.

Faye shook her head. "No. Leaves a bad taste in their mouth," she smirked. Faye looked down at the walking staff and picked it up. Aside from the claw marks showing an attempt to pop out the diamonds, the four jewels were still in place. She held onto the staff tightly.

"*Faye, is that—?*" Rinji asked. She only nodded as a tear ran down her cheek. A deep, comforting growl came from the dragon as he nuzzled her shoulder with his snout. "*I am sure he is fine, Faye. But you should keep going. Even though a deal was made, Kay-Tahs aren't to be trusted,*" he warned.

Faye nodded. "*We will see you in Arana, my friend.*" Rinji took off into the air without waiting another moment.

Tristan came forward and observed the walking

staff in Faye's hand. He placed a reassuring hand on her shoulder. "We'll find him," he whispered.

"So, those Kay-Tahs were people from your village," Zachariah noted out loud. "How did the other High Sorcerers take that when they found out?" he asked.

Tristan climbed onto his horse, a serious look on his face. "They never found out, and for personal reasons, I'd like to keep it that way."

Zachariah nodded, still staring at the High Sorcerer. Faye knew the huntsman was curious.

So was she.

CHAPTER FIFTEEN: THE STORIES

AFTER TWO DAYS OF TRAVELING, THEY MADE IT TO A VILLAGE JUST OUTSIDE OF ARANA. Although the sun had just set, Princess Dara and Faye once again donned their hooded cloaks to conceal their faces. The village was not only surrounded by merchants, but guards as well. They followed Tristan quietly into an inn.

"Wait here," he ordered the three as he went to the innkeeper. After a few moments passed, he returned with a reassuring smirk on his face. "Okay, we have two rooms, only..."

"Only what?" Zachariah raised an eyebrow. Faye imagined him growling under his silk cover... His scars moving with the shape his mouth was making as he spoke... she shook her head and focused on Tristan.

Tristan cleared his throat nervously. "They only had *two* rooms left...each with one bed. And in order to obtain these rooms, I had to assure the old man we were...together."

Faye raised an eyebrow. "Together?" she echoed. "What, as in...?"

Tristan casually wrapped his arm around her shoulder. "Together." From the corner of her eye, Faye saw the fire in Zachariah's eyes, as if they were burning Tristan's very soul. She was going to say something when Tristan began pulling her closer. "Ah, here is the Innkeeper now, darling!" he announced loudly as a taller, scrawny man with short black hair and glasses on the bridge of his nose appeared. "We are ready, good sir."

The Innkeeper nodded as he led the four up the stairs. Princess Dara held onto Zachariah's hand while Tristan continued to have his arm wrapped around Faye's shoulder. Faye put on a smile and pretended to act happy and in love.

"Faye?" Rinji's voice echoed in her mind. "*I can feel your emotions running wild. Is something happening?*"

The young girl blushed at the invasion in her thoughts. "*Rinji! I thought there was too much distance between us!*"

"No, child. I am at the outskirts of the woods in case those trolls try anything." The Innkeeper led Zachariah and the cloaked Princess to their room, and just a few rooms down was the room Faye and Tristan would occupy.

"Tristan and I are apparently pretending to be...together. All this Innkeeper had was two rooms; each with one bed, " Faye thought through gritted teeth, her heart beating faster. There was silence for a moment as Tristan thanked the Innkeeper, tipped him and closed the door.

"I know you want it to be real," Rinji uttered. Faye let out a shriek, then quickly covered her mouth. Tristan raised an eyebrow and smiled.

"Something Rinji said?" he laughed softly. Faye shook her head.

"I—I thought I saw a mouse, or something," she lied horribly. "So," she cleared her throat, "how much enjoyment did you take from that act?"

Tristan tilted his head. "Act?"

"Putting your arm around me, seeing Zachariah cringe—"

Tristan laughed. "Yes, it's always amusing seeing his reactions. Well, *half* of his reactions," he corrected himself, using his hand to cover the bottom half of his face mockingly.

Faye smiled. "Well, thank goodness it's only pretend," she said softly.

There was a silence that lingered in the room for a while. Tristan nodded. "Yes, thank goodness. Tell me, how did you become in acquaintance with him, anyway?"

Faye stared down at her fingers. "Fate, actually. It was when I first started living with Marcus," she sighed. "I had developed my...my 'Gift'—of magic, not—well, you know..." she gestured towards her back. "Anyway," she chuckled softly, "I had developed my Gift a lot before living with him. When my parents died, I was devastated. I felt so alone, despite Marcus' attempts to help. I decided I would run away late one night, leave Janulai and just survive with my magic. What I didn't know back then was that my magic was useless when it came to water." Faye remembered the cold rain hitting her face as she ran into the woods. "I-I tried making shade out of the branches but I didn't know how to do anything without magic.

"The rain poured harder than usual that night. I was cold, tired and hungry, not to mention completely lost. I tried finding my way back, but tripped, and," Faye blinked a few times, looking up at the curious Sorcerer, "the next thing I know, I was in this hut..."

***

"Are you alright?" a concerned voice asked. Faye looked around at the unfamiliar surroundings; the bed was small but long and covered in animal fur as a blanket. There was a small fire in the corner underneath her wet green robe. When she noticed, she pulled her blanket around herself tighter and looked to her right. The man, although he was sitting, was taller than she was, with long blond hair that just passed his shoulders, and a silk scarf covering the bottom half of his face. His pointed ears poked just past his hair.

"You're an Elf!" she gasped in awe, coughing a little. The Elf glanced around nervously.

"I'm sorry, miss," the stranger hesitated, "You were lost in the woods, crying for help. Then you fell and hit your head. I couldn't very well leave you to die. You could have gotten—" he hesitated when Faye sneezed into the crook of her elbow, coughing slightly. "...sick. Well, too late for that, I suppose," he sighed. The stranger got up, his back now toward the sick Sorceress. When he turned around, he had a bowl and spoon. "Eat. This will warm you up in no time," he offered. Faye hesitated at first, but then looked into his eyes. They were so calm and concerned, she couldn't help but smile softly at the Elf as she took the bowl.

"Thank you, erm..?"

"Oh, forgive me," he laughed nervously, "I'm not used to having guests. I'm Zachariah, huntsman to the Elven Clan of the Four Kingdoms."

Faye sniffled. "I'm Faye. W-We have an Elven Clan?"

"Well, we travel everywhere and visit the four Kingdoms. We live mostly in the forests so as to not get in the way of humans. But when I saw you needed help, I couldn't leave you."

Faye nodded. "I'm Faye, and I'm in your debt, Zachariah,"

He shook his head. "Your friendship is all I would truly desire."

***

"It took me awhile to get healthy again," Faye recalled, "but after that, we couldn't stop seeing each other. He showed me the forest in ways I would never have imagined. He showed me how to hunt, navigate, and hide in plain sight. All without using magic."

Tristan nodded. "So, he isn't a fan of magic. Do you know why?" Tristan asked. Faye shook her head.

That was one thing she didn't truly know.

"All I know is that Elves do not care for using too much magic," she replied. "They only use it for little things."

"Like how to fly?" Tristan raised an eyebrow. Faye blushed, not saying anything. "Right. Well, if it's all the same to you, I shall take this pillow and top blanket and sleep on the floor. You take the bed," he insisted. Faye nodded climbing slowly into the bed, a feeling of guilt and sadness invading her mind. Just then, Tristan walked over and tucked her in. She smiled.

"No one's ever tucked me in before," she whispered, their faces inches apart from each other.

"What, your parents never...?"

Faye shook her head. "If they did, I don't remember. They died when I was younger."

Tristan sighed. "I'm sorry, you just said that. I wasn't...I didn't—"

"No, no...it's okay, really," Faye reassured the High Sorcerer. She gazed into his eyes; his curious brown eyes with a special hint of gold dancing through them. "What about you? Where are your parents?" she asked.

He sighed. "It's—It's complicated." He sat on the edge of the bed. "Damn," he laughed. "I can't lie to you. I don't know why....maybe it's your eyes," he guessed out loud, staring at Faye. "You actually met my parents already."

Faye looked at Tristan in shock. Did she already meet his parents? "No, I don't think I—"

"My mother gave you that staff," he said softly as he pointed at the walking staff. Faye's eyes glanced over to the staff, then back to Tristan. Her jaw dropped at the realization.

"Lor-Lor?!"

"Lor-Lor."

There was silence for a few moments. Then, Faye chuckled loudly.

"What's so funny?" Tristan asked.

"I called your mom a 'he', threatened her life with Rinji, and told you to 'shut it'. I'm making *great* first impressions on you and your family so far!" she laughed. In a few moments, Tristan joined in and laughed with her, the harmonies of their laughter probably echoing through the halls, but she didn't care. As the laughter died down, she caught her breath. There was a long pause as Faye stared at the candle burning brightly on the nightstand.

"My parents died in a fire," she recalled. "The fire wasn't your normal fire, though...the flames were purple and black." Faye saw Tristan tense up as she told him. "I don't know what my family did to deserve that. But I've seen her, that Milla Sorceress," tears slowly filled her eyes, but she blinked them away. "I've seen her twice now, in my sleep. The first time was days before the King died. The second was in the palace, when I apparently passed out."

"Thankfully I caught you, or you'd have an injury," Tristan blurted out. Faye stared at him. He winked playfully at her. "Well, in my defense, I did tell you I would have hated to see that pretty head of yours hit the floor," he nodded. "Anyway, it's late. We need to get sleep." Without warning, he kissed her forehead, causing Faye to blush slightly. "Goodnight, Dragon Whisperer."

***

"Faye! Faye, wake up!"

The young Sorceress shot up from bed, out of breath as tears started streaming down her cheeks. She grabbed her arms and shoulders in panic. "The-the fire. There was a fire, and I could feel everything. I s-saw them die....my p-parents, M-Marcus," she began to cry. "Tristan, her eyes...her eyes—"

Tristan climbed into the bed and with one easy swoop, both were under the covers as he held her. Faye sobbed uncontrollably. The nightmare felt painfully real. "It was a nightmare," he assured the sobbing girl as he calmly shushed her. "You are safe. I will never let anything happen to you, Faye." He combed his fingers through her short red hair. The sobbing quieted after a while, yet Tristan never released his hold. She felt safe and protected in his arms, listening to his steady breathing as she drifted into a peaceful sleep.

***

The next time Faye woke up, it was morning. She didn't remember the last time she had slept so peacefully. She turned her head to the left and saw Tristan sleeping beside her, still holding her. His breathing was slow and steady. When he opened his eyes, she suddenly felt embarrassed for staring.

"Morning," she whispered.

Tristan smiled softly. "Morning. No more nightmares?" Faye shook her head. "Good, I'm glad."

"We should get going," Faye suggested.

"Oh, I agree."

Neither one moved. Faye giggled. "So, are you going to get up?"

Tristan hesitated at first, then suddenly there was a knock at the door. "I guess I have no choice now," he sighed. As he rose from bed, Faye smiled. She was relieved to have most of the night without any dreams involving amethyst eyes. "Thank you, sir," she heard Tristan say as he closed the door. When he turned around, he revealed a tray that had two mugs and two plates of eggs, grits, and fresh fruit. "Breakfast?" he offered Faye as he sat back in bed.

Faye looked at the arrangement of food, her stomach softly growling in appreciation. "Wha—when was this set up?" she asked in shock.

"Early this morning," Tristan answered, grabbing a fresh strawberry and taking a bite. "I assume Zachariah and the Princess are receiving the same thing. Let's eat. We still have a bit of traveling to do before we get to the Palace."

***

The four met outside the inn. Faye turned around and smiled when she saw the name on the sign. "The Rustic Spoon," she commented. "Quite the name for—" she stopped mid-sentence when she spotted a familiar face in the crowds. Although the figure was disguised in a different outfit, she'd recognize those caramel eyes anywhere. "Um, I want to look around the marketplace before we officially head out," Faye announced.

"That sounds like a marvelous idea," Princess Dara agreed. The men shrugged their shoulders, but Tristan looked especially annoyed.

"Fine," he muttered, "but make it quick." Faye smiled at the others as she hurried away, pretending to gawk and admire the trinkets being sold. She hurried around the corner, scanning the crowd for the familiar face. Marcus was here somewhere, she just had to look. Suddenly, she felt a hand cover her mouth and pull her into the shadows. She tried fighting the figure off until she was forced to turn around. Marcus smiled weakly at her, a shadow of a beard forming around his jawline. His caramel eyes looked tired but relieved as he pulled her into a loving hug.

"Faye," he whispered, a sigh of relief escaping his lips, "thank goodness you're okay." Faye didn't want to let go, but eventually did, blinking away tears.

"You left me," she whispered. "You—you said nothing! You just up and left me alone! So much has—"

"Faye," he interrupted her. His voice trembled and his eyes were cold and fearful. "You shouldn't have come here. It's not safe for you. Hell, it isn't even safe for *me*. You have no idea what I'm risking right now just talking to you."

Faye stared at him with mixed feelings of shock and anger. "I...I left Janulai. I came looking for you! Being chased by the *Varjo*, seeing a Sorceress with amethyst eyes, meeting my dragon and receiving my Mark—"

Marcus covered her mouth quickly, frantically looking around. "Not so loud, you fool!" he hissed. "Shadows are everywhere...hidden in the darkness, hearing every word." He released his grasp, fear showing in his eyes. "You have no idea the trouble that lies ahead. I tried protecting you from her, tried keeping your Gift a secret. Somehow, she figured it out..." he mumbled something under his breath, frantically looking around as if someone else was watching them.

"Marcus, I don't—"

"You have to let me go, Faye," Marcus ordered. "I'm trouble. I only risked this encounter because I wanted to tell you," he hesitated before grabbing her shoulders, "You were the only good thing to happen in my life. I loved you like my own flesh and blood and would do *anything* to keep you safe. I never meant for things to be like this; it was *never* supposed to be like this. I was supposed to—" There was a sudden burst of wind as purple and black smoke whirled around the two. Faye looked around in panic as Marcus shoved her out of the circle. "Get out of here, Faye!" he yelled. The mass morphed into two beings, each with hooded cloaks and amethyst eyes.

"The Varjo," Faye thought to herself. "Marcus, NO!" she cried. One of the *Varjo* looked at her direction, his amethyst eyes shining brighter and a smile forming across his face. Marcus punched one square in the jaw and shot an energy ball at the other. Soon, more took their place, holding Marcus down.

"She is waiting for you, Jaako," one of the *Varjo* hissed. He looked at Faye, not afraid anymore, but calm as he closed his eyes and became engulfed in the purple and black smoke. In that second, as Faye tried to run to his aide, the mass disappeared, leaving no trace of Marcus or the *Varjo*. Faye collapsed to the ground and cried.

Just like that, Marcus was gone once more. So many questions raced through Faye's mind. What was he going to say before they took him? Who was Jaako?

"Faye, you have to calm your mind. You are going so fast," Rinji commented.

"I saw Marcus."

"What?! When?!"

"Just now. The Varjo took him. He was going to say something before..." Faye began to cry once more.

"You have to tell the others," Rinji suggested. *"Tristan, or even the Princess. They might be able to help. You can't do*

180

this alone. You shouldn't have to go through this alone."

"Emma, don't!" a younger voice called. Faye whirled around and saw two little girls standing behind her, peeking around the corner of the building. They had short, dark hair, blue eyes, and dirt on their faces. Their clothes were torn, and they had nothing to cover their feet.

Feeling disheveled, Faye quickly wiped the tears from her face and put on a small smile. "Hello there," she said softly. "Are you lost?"

The girls shook their head, looking at each other uneasily and hurried off. Faye followed them, curious to see where they were going. She saw them peeking over a merchant's cart that served fresh fruit. The merchant growled at the kids, telling them to go away.

"No money, no food!" he barked at the girls. Faye brushed her hair behind her ears and walked calmly over to the merchant's cart.

"Excuse me, sir. Are these melons fresh?" she asked.

The merchant's eyes lit up at the sight of a customer. "Yes, ma'am! Freshest in the land!" he exclaimed with a dazzling smile.

"I'll buy two of your largest melons, please. Oh, and some of that bread you have, too." The merchant hurried to retrieve the items Faye requested. She happily paid the man, and while still there, Faye knelt down to the children and gave them the food. "Here you go, girls. Go on, take it," she motioned for them to take the food, ignoring the grumbling rising from the merchant. After a few moments, the girls took the food, thanked Faye, and hurried off.

"Why would you do that?!" The merchant asked. "I gave you my best melons and you wasted them!"

"You got your money," Faye growled. "You should be happy about that," she spat as she stormed away, leaving the merchant speechless. As she walked through the marketplace once more, she spotted the Princess gazing at the jewelry and decided to join her. "See anything interesting?" she asked, peering over the Princess' shoulder. Dara turned to smile, then showed concern.

"Faye, were you crying?" she inquired. Faye stared at the Princess uneasily. "Oh, forgive me, it is none of my concern," she quickly said, suddenly showing her a bracelet woven out of horsehair. "How natural!" she complimented. Faye smirked until she felt a tug on her cloak. Looking down, she saw the younger of the two sisters with a smile and small driblets of melon juice on her face.

"Hello, there—Emma, is it?" Faye asked. The little

girl nodded, then handed her a necklace made out of flowers. "Is that for me?" Faye gasped. The little girl's smile grew bigger as she nodded, pointing just ahead of them. When Faye looked up, she saw the older sister and their mother. The mother smiled at Faye, her eyes looking like she was crying as she mouthed a silent thank you.

"Thank you, *Basilla*," Emma said softly as she skipped away.

Faye hesitated, but quickly followed the little girl. "Wait!" she tried to call softly. "What did you—Oh, hello, ma'am," she stopped when she realized she was in front of their mother. She had deep blue eyes and long, brown hair that was tied with a red bandanna. "I'm sorry to come over here like this, but your daughter...she called me..."

"*Basilla*," the little girl finished. "Mommy, I knew it was her. She helped the poor, just like you said the *Basilla Fafner* would!" she exclaimed with a grin. "This is my sister, Rebekkah. She didn't believe me when I said you were the *Basilla*, but I knew it! I did! She's just like in the stories with the purple smoke and everything!"

"Emma, please...go play with your sister," their mother whispered calmly. The two children followed orders and headed off, but not before Emma gave Faye a surprising hug.

"Thank you, *Basilla*," she whispered sweetly before running off. The mother looked at Faye, laughing nervously.

"What did she mean, 'stories'?" Faye asked the mother.

The mother glanced around uneasily and motioned for her to come closer. "Stories, legends, what have you... have been told all across the four Kingdoms. The stories say that the Dragon Whisperers would come out of hiding once the *Basilla Fafner* — protector of dragons and mankind — showed himself...and that the *Basilla Fafner* would bring us out of the darkness. My little one, Emma," she chuckled, "always said there would be a girl Dragon Whisperer, despite the stories."

Faye chuckled softly. She reached inside her pocket and gave the mother a few more coins. "It's not much, but at least you can get yourself a decent meal. Take care of yourself and your little ones, and—" she gasped sharply as she felt a sharp, burning sensation in her shoulder blade. "R-Rinji—"

"Faye! The Varjo found me! I need to lead them away from the village! I—" The pain struck her again, causing her to cry out. Tears streamed down her cheeks as she

pictured a dagger being dug into her skin, the hot steel twisting inside her flesh. Faye collapsed to the ground in pain as she grabbed for the knife in her shoulder blade, finding nothing but air.

"They're hurting him!" Faye cried out as she slammed her fist onto the ground.

"Miss," the mother knelt down beside her, placing a hand unknowingly onto the very spot that caused pain. "You're burning! Rebekkah! I need a wet cloth, now!" Faye could feel the mother try to remove her hooded cloak and weakly tried to stop her.

"No, please," she whispered. "Leave him alone," she muttered. She could feel the mother successfully pull down the hooded cloak and white shirt; the cool breeze that entered their hut flowing over her newly exposed Mark. She heard the mother gasp loudly and back away. Faye felt the strength return to her tenfold as she heard Rinji's roar come from the direction of the woods.

"*I-I'm alright,*" Rinji's voice assured her. "*Just a small wound. Don't go through the woods again! Follow the river!*" he warned. Faye looked at the mother, her blue eyes lit with wonder and surprise. Without saying another word, Faye ran out of the hut.

"Dragon Whisperer! It *is* you!" Faye heard the mother cry out and hesitated. A few nearby merchants overheard the mother's cry and hurried to Faye, all of them touching her cloak and holding her hands.

"Dragon Whisperer!"

"Will you save us?"

"I knew the stories were true..."

Their voices were overlapping as she tried to get away before Guards overheard the chatter and came...or worse, the *Varjo*. In that moment, she felt someone grab her arm forcefully out of the crowd.

"I hope you're done shopping," Tristan growled, his eyes narrowing as he stared down at her.

CHAPTER SIXTEEN: THE SOUTHERN KING

WHAT WERE YOU THINKING?" Tristan's eyes narrowed down at the young Sorceress as he and the others hurried out of the marketplace. "Are you trying to get yourself killed?! The *Varjo* have your scent now. They know where you are! We have no choice now but to speak to her..." he grumbled to himself.

"Who? Tristan, what are you talking about?" Princess Dara asked.

Tristan groaned aloud as they headed back to the Rusty Spoon to retrieve their horses. "King Danyll of Arana is one of the youngest Kings alive. Since he is a...youthful King...Listerah, mother and Queen Regent, speaks 'on behalf of the King,'" he explained as he rolled his eyes. "But first we must see Lord Godebeer, the

King's uncle. He's the reason I'm hardly inside the palace walls, unlike the other High Sorcerers and *their* Kings."

"Well, surely they will let a Princess in," Dara countered. "We will have no problem. Now let us get ready." Faye, despite Dara's attempt at halting her by grabbing her cloak, rushed towards Tristan.

"Listen, I'm sorry for worrying you," Faye apologized, trying to follow behind the irritated High Sorcerer.

Tristan spun around and leaned towards her. "'Worry' doesn't begin to describe what I was feeling," Tristan whispered, inches from the young girl's face.

Zachariah defensively wedged himself between the two Sorcerers. "Walk away, Sorcerer," Zachariah warned.

The High Sorcerer laughed dryly as he readied his horse."You are so irresponsible, Faye! You don't care about anything—"

"I saw Marcus."

The group froze as the three were about to mount their horses. "That's right," Faye continued, "I saw him. He came to warn me about something, but the *Varjo* arrived and took him before I could do anything. They even *looked* in my direction, but still did nothing to me! I was right this whole time: Marcus is alive. I don't care what you think of me...Marcus is in trouble, and—"

Tristan held up a hand and Faye took that as a moment to breathe. "What...*exactly*...did they do?" he asked, a little calmer than before.

Faye fiddled with the flower crown gift she received as she recalled the incident. "They grabbed him. I-I tried to stop them," she ignored Zachariah's disappointed stare, "and-and he got rid of the two, but more took their place." Her brows furrowed at the last thing she heard. "They called him, 'Jaako'. He was going to tell me something he was supposed to do and now I'll never know."

Zachariah raised an eyebrow. "Jaako? What is that supposed to mean?"

"Doesn't matter now," Tristan replied, getting on his horse. "We have to speak to Lord Godebeer about this. If we leave now, we can make it to the palace by nightfall."

"We need to follow the river," Faye informed the three. "Rinji says the woods aren't safe. He ran into some *Varjo*."

Princess Dara hesitated and glanced up at Zachariah. "I-I'm sure they'll be gone, since it sounds like they only came for—"

"—but they could come back for Faye," Zachariah argued.

"If they wanted me, they would have taken me then...it was like I wasn't even there to them."

"Enough," Tristan interrupted. "We follow the river. Get on your horses."

***

The ride to the palace was a silent one. Faye rode on the back of Zachariah's horse this time, holding onto his waist as they followed the quiet Selti River and rode toward the high palace walls. She peered over the huntsman's shoulder and admired the fortress. No one could possibly sneak in; there were about twenty guards surrounding the gates, and two more in front of the travelers. Archers paced the walls, their sharp eyes scanning the area for anything suspicious, and right now, their eyes — and arrows — were aimed at them.

"Halt!" One of the guards barked. "What business do you have here?"

Tristan let out a soft sigh. "Really?" he muttered. Faye watched the guard's face as it went from protective to shocked in a matter of seconds.

"Oh! H-High Sorcerer Tristan! Forgive me, sir! I did not know—"

"No, you didn't," Tristan retorted. He motioned to the group behind him. "They're with me. We're here to see His Royal Majesty. Or the Queen Regent. Just not Good Bear."

"Lord Godebeer, you mean…" the guard corrected, suddenly looking away. Faye couldn't see the look Tristan was giving the panicked guard but she imagined it was one not to be meddled with. "I mean, o-of course! Let them pass immediately!" When the gate began to lift, Tristan nodded at the guards as they passed by. On the other side of the gate, Faye noticed that things were just as heavily guarded inside.

"Ah, Tristan!" a voice called from above. Faye glanced up and saw a man dressed in blue and silver patterned clothes. His head was completely bald, and his eyes stared down at Tristan, an odd smile showing on his face. "We didn't think you'd ever return."

"Sorry to disappoint you, Good Bear," Tristan slid off his horse and bowed, the others following suit.

The man's smile shrunk. "It's Godebeer. How many times must I tell you? Godebeer!" He hissed.

"Always once more, sir." Tristan replied innocently. Faye couldn't help but smirk as she watched Godebeer squirm with impatience. "Anyway, we are here on important matters and need to speak to the King—"

"Unfortunately, the King is quite busy," Godebeer interrupted Tristan, shrugging his shoulders.

"Why am I not surprised?" Tristan countered. Faye glanced over at Zachariah and Princess Dara, both having the same blank expression, remaining silent. "Well then, perhaps the Queen Regent—"

"Busy as well, it seems. But fear not, you may tell me and I will decide if it is important enough for the King or Queen Regent to hear."

"I believe I can make *that* decision on my own, Lord Godebeer," a voice responded. Faye watched as the guards suddenly stood at attention while Tristan, Zachariah, the Princess and Lord Godebeer bowed before King Danyll. His face showed he was no older than thirteen, Faye guessed, his brilliant yellow hair peeking underneath his elaborate crown, decorated in beautiful gems of all colors and sizes. His eyes were a brilliant blue, and suddenly locked onto Faye's curious green eyes. Realizing she was staring at royalty, she immediately broke eye contact and curtsied, staring at the ground as her cheeks grew hot.

"Tristan!" the King exclaimed. "It has been far too long...a year?"

"About that long, Your Majesty," Tristan replied.

"Please rise, good friends of Tristan," the King

requested. "Anyone that is a friend to this brave man here is *more* than welcome inside my castle."

"Erm, sire," Lord Godebeer cleared his throat. "The one covered by the silk scarf—"

"Is with me, as well," Tristan interrupted. "Which makes him welcome."

"Come! We have much to discuss. You must be hungry!" The youthful King insisted. As they followed, Tristan hurried over to Zachariah.

"No matter what, do not tell them what you are. Do not speak unless directly spoken to," Tristan ordered in hushed tones. Faye saw the look of anger and confusion in Zachariah's eyes. "Your very life might depend on it," Tristan explained as the four entered the Throne Room.

What the Throne Room lacked in blue and silver tapestries, it made up for with weaponry of all shapes and sizes. Metal decorated the palace walls; sheilds, swords, bows and arrows of all kinds. Faye gulped nervously, glancing over to Zachariah, his facial expression mirroring her own. Princess Dara, on the other hand, seemed to be enthralled.

"What an amazing collection, Your Highness." the Princess complimented as the doors closed behind them.

"Your Highness, may I present Princess Daralis of

Salzar," Tristan formerly introduced, "only daughter of the late King Leonus."

Dara curtsied once more. "Your Highness."

The King approached the Princess, a look of curiosity in his young eyes. "Princess Daralis, I'm sorry about the passing of King Leonus. I was told he was a good King."

"He was, your Grace," the Princess responded. "I could have learned more from him."

"As I imagine we all could have," King Danyll admitted. Suddenly, the door opened, revealing a beautiful woman with long blonde hair curled past her shoulders. Her dress was a deep shade of blue with lace layering over it, and was long enough for the lace to drag on the polished floor.

"The Queen Regent," a guard announced from the doorway. Everyone bowed as she approached the small group. Faye peeked up and saw how extravagant the Queen Regent looked; her body was slim, her skin was like porcelain, and her lips were as red as the deepest rose. Her smile was small yet sincere.

"Tristan," she sighed, pulling him into a hug. "It has been a while."

"Yes it has, Queen Regent," Tristan nodded before clearing his throat. "Princess Dara, may I present

Listerah Stonewall; mother of our King Danyll and Queen Regent of Arana."

Listerah held onto the Princess' hands, a look of sadness in her eyes. "I loved your father, King Leonus. He was a good father and strong King. If you ever need anything, please—"

"Actually, Your Grace," Dara motioned toward Faye. "There is."

The Queen Regent glanced over to Faye and nodded. "Danyll, go back to your studies please." The young King looked as if he wanted to protest, but one glance from his mother and he nodded silently.

"Don't leave without a proper goodbye this time, Tristan," the King commanded.

Tristan smiled at the young King and nodded in return. "As you command, my King."

When the King left, Listerah glanced over at Faye and the huntsman. "Who are you two?" she asked, staring more at Zachariah.

"Oh! I'm Faye Haybear of Janulai, Queen Regent," the young Sorceress curtsied awkwardly. When she looked up, she noticed a hint of amusement in the Queen Regent's eyes. "This is Zachariah, my most trusted friend and huntsman."

Zachariah bowed gracefully. "I heard stories of your

beauty, but it seems the stories do not come anywhere close to the real thing."

Listerah smiled and politely bowed her head in acknowledgement. "Welcome to Arana, friends of Tristan. Now, what brings you here?"

Faye started at the beginning, when Marcus disappeared. She watched the Queen Regent's facial expressions change from shocked, to angry, to sad, and to calm with every new piece of information given, including the false treaty that was now in the Queen Regent's hands.

"You've gone through so much in so little time, Dragon Whisperer," Listerah observed loudly, after taking in the information. She eyed Zachariah, her brows furrowing as if she was solving a puzzle. "You're part of the Elven Clan, aren't you?" she finally asked, her eyes suddenly cold.

Zachariah hesitated. He glanced over at Tristan uneasily before looking back at the Queen Regent. "Yes, Your Majesty."

Listerah nodded. "Thank you for your honesty. Tristan must have warned you about not telling me what you are," she assumed, glancing at the guilty Sorcerer. "Well, he had every right to be afraid for your safety. Normally, I would have you killed on the spot for even being here."

Zachariah's brows furrowed. "Because I'm—"

"Long ago, when my late husband ruled Arana, and was still a new King," the Queen Regent walked to one of the walls and played with the tapestry that hung low, "there was a battle. Not a grand battle memorialized in stories, mind you, but still a battle nonetheless. We had our weapons, an aspect our land is still well known for. But this...*army*...they had a magic that was unlike anything my husband had ever seen. He called for help anywhere he could, even reaching out to your King, Arvellon." Zachariah tensed at the name, but said nothing. "They witnessed the dark magic, and he refused to help—HE REFUSED. Oh, we were victorious, yes...but no thanks to your kind. We still lost many...too many. I remember the anger in his eyes at the betrayal of those...creatures," her hands tightened on the bottom of the tapestry until it finally fell to the ground. "I will not have that happen again. You come, asking for our help while you have *him* traveling with you?! Do you mean to insult me, Tristan?!" she yelled while glaring at the High Sorcerer. "My son's ruling should be just, and right...there is nothing right about him," Listerah cried, pointing towards the huntsman.

"That was all before my time, Queen Regent,"

Zachariah countered. "I was too young to even hold a bow when that travesty occurred!"

"Are you raising your voice at me?" the Queen Regent challenged. "Remember who you are speaking to."

Zachariah marched over to the angered Queen. "All I see is a human holding a grudge. If I could blame you for things your kind did to *us*, wouldn't *you* call it unjust since you weren't there?" In one swift moment, he removed his silk scarf and watched as the Queen Regent hesitated, yet her eyes continued staring at the scars that marked his face. "*This* is what *your kind* did to *me*. They tortured me, sliced my face with their daggers, but not before dousing them in flames! As I screamed in pain, they drank their ale and watched me suffer. I remember wanting to die. Yet here I stand, with Faye by my side as trusted friend and companion. I would give my life to keep her safe, even if *you* do not wish to help."

Faye's jaw dropped. This was one story she did not know about her friend. Her heart ached for him, imagining what he went through before their paths had crossed.

The Queen Regent's mouth formed a stern line. "Master Tristan," she stared at the High Sorcerer, her icy glare matching the tone in her voice, "your group asks me for my help, and I appreciate the courtesy…"

She fiddled with the treaty, her fingers tracing over Salzar's wax seal. With one swift movement, the queen lifted it towards one of the flaming torches, burning the treaty into ashes. "But as long as you are traveling with *him*," her glare shifted for a split second towards Zachariah as she finished her thought with a much louder tone, "my answer is no. I'm sure you can see your own way out."

Tristan groaned softly under his breath as he nodded in understanding. "Yes, Queen Regent." Several guards swiftly entered the Throne Room and surrounded the group. Tristan looked over to Faye, a solemn expression on his face as the troupe was escorted out.

"You can't blame yourself, Zachariah," Princess Dara assured him, placing a hand on his shoulder. He looked to her and nodded, as he held onto her hand. Faye couldn't help but feel a sudden pang inside at the simple gesture.

"This isn't the first time someone blamed me for something I didn't do," he sighed softly as he covered his face with the silk scarf once more.

"Don't," Dara pleaded. "Leave it off." Faye watched as Dara took the scarf, and handed it to her noncha- lantly. "Faye, put this away."

Instead of doing what she was told, Faye held onto the scarf, feeling the silk rub against her fingers. She always wondered what was hidden underneath this simple piece of fabric, but now realized that things — like the scars — were more complex than she ever thought possible.

Before she realized it, Faye left the group and stormed back into the room, barely hearing Tristan's warnings. "Queen Regent!" she blurted out. The Queen's surprised look only paused Faye for a brief moment. "If you do this, you're no better than them."

Listerah's lips formed another stern line as the fire in her eyes grew. "What did you just say?"

"You said you want your son's ruling to be just, and right. Well, how is *this* just? How is this right?! Turning others away that need your help. You're no better than that Elven King that ignored your late husband's plea."

"My Queen," a voice called. Faye whirled around and saw Lord Godebeer standing in the doorway, accompanied by three guards, each of them with weapons in hand.

"Oh, for goodness sake, Godebeer! Call off your dogs, they're not needed here," Queen Listerah groaned in annoyance. After a moment's pause, she raised an eyebrow at the young Sorceress, a curious smirk on her face. "Or *are* they? The choice is yours, Faye. Don't be so naive in your response." Queen Listerah reached for Faye's hair, brushing it behind her ear. "You're just a child. What do you know about the world? Go back to Janulai. The world isn't safe for children to wander."

Faye stared up at the elegant Queen, her face stern but her eyes lit with fire. Angered, Faye nodded silently and slowly walked away. Godebeer and his guards made a small opening for her to pass through. Her eyes locked onto Tristan's and she could feel her cheeks heating up.

"Faye," Rinji's voice echoed in her mind. Ignoring it, she stormed past the three travelers until someone grabbed her arm. She felt a sudden sense of frustration and worry as she looked up at Zachariah's concerned gaze. She couldn't help but trace her line of vision around the scars surrounding his mouth, then back up to his eyes, and wondered who would be so cruel to cause someone such harm.

"Faye, answer me!" Rinji's voice commanded.

"Faye, it'll be alright," Zachariah assured the young girl, but she was still too upset.

"No, it won't," she muttered, placing the silk scarf in Zachariah's hand. As he slowly placed the silk scarf on, once more covering the lower half of his face, she suddenly felt a rush of anger build inside her. Faye gasped softly and grabbed her chest; she felt like she wanted to hurt everyone standing in the immediate area of her as she screamed at the top of her lungs. Her knees felt weak as she stumbled to the ground.

"Faye! What's wrong?" Zachariah asked, his voice filled with worry.

Before anything else could be said, screaming was heard from outside. Lord Godebeer and his guards hurried outside, carrying their swords defensively. Immediately following was the young King Danyll.

"Tristan!" he shouted excitedly, looking at the High Sorcerer. "A dragon is trying to attack the palace walls!"

Faye's heart dropped. She pushed herself off the ground, stumbled a few steps, and hurried after the guards and Lord Godebeer, ignoring the excited shouts from the guards as they armed themselves with more weapons. As her eyes adjusted to the blinding sunlight, she saw the shimmering green and yellow scales of Rinji as he gave a tremendous roar, his throat beginning to glow a soft orange.

The young Sorceress ran past the guards, trying to get to Rinji before flames touched the ground. "NO! RINJI!"

Rinji's eyes locked onto hers. The orange glow emitting from his chest and throat soon faded away, his eyes never leaving her. Relief coursed through Faye's body, and she wasn't sure if it was her feeling relief for Rinji or the other way around. She suddenly heard a guard shout, feeling someone grab her by the waist and attempt to pull her away. "No! Let me go!" she cried, as she started clawing at the armored arms in attempt to fight off the guard. Enraged, Faye's hands glowed a brilliant green as she grabbed onto the guard's hands, who suddenly cried out in pain.

The guard released his grip, giving Faye a chance to hurry to Rinji. She threw a large energy ball, which was bigger than her fist, at the ground. The area began to shake with enough force to crack, dividing her and Rinji from everyone else. The void itself was nearly five feet wide and curved away from Faye. Her eyes locked onto Lord Godebeer, who was cowering behind a group of guards.

"Call off your dogs, Godebeer," Faye hissed. To the left of Godebeer were a group of guards arming what looked like a giant crossbow pointed directly at Rinji. The dragon's throat glowed a brilliant orange before he released a fireball the size of a large boulder towards the weapon, causing it to burst into flames. The soldiers scattered away from the fire and made a protective ring around the King and Lord Godebeer. A threatening growl was heard from Rinji's throat as he protectively wrapped his tail in front of the young Sorceress.

"Call...them...*off!*" Faye growled once more. Godebeer, who had turned pale, raised a shaky hand. The guards slowly sheathed their swords once more. "You're so quick to protect your own," Faye scoffed, "but you won't help your neighboring lands that are in need of weaponry, and a good defense like you have?"

"Faye, calm down," Tristan warned, motioning to her hands. When she looked down, she noticed they were glowing a fierce purple.

"Where does this keep coming from?" she thought to herself as she made the color fade away. She glanced back up at the King Danyll and Godebeer; while Godebeer's face showed nothing but fear and nausea, the young King's eyes were fixated on the dragon, a small smile creeping onto his face.

"He's intrigued by you," Faye thought to Rinji. As she communicated this, the King slowly walked past the guards and headed for Faye and Rinji, stopping at the large chasm. Faye glanced over at Lord Godebeer, then back at Tristan, who only nodded silently. *"If he tries—"*

"Godebeer is too much of a coward to try anything," Rinji nuzzled his snout against her shoulder, carefully guiding Faye away from the chasm she created. She

suddenly felt calm and watched Rinji as he slowly stretched his long neck across the void until his snout was inches from the King. *"Let him know I won't hurt him,"* Rinji suggested.

"I think he knows you won't hurt him," she spoke aloud, eyeing the King. King Danyll extended his hand slowly, hesitant at first. Still not touching Rinji, his excited eyes locked onto Faye, then behind him towards his guards. Rinji inched closer until his snout made contact with the King's hand. King Danyll gasped and jumped softly, and Faye noticed the excitement and curiosity increase in his eyes.

Sadly, it only lasted a moment.

Just behind the King, a spear was thrown in their direction. Faye could feel the anger burning inside her once more as Rinji let out a loud growl, nudging the King out of the way and blocking Faye with his large tail. Scared for Rinji's safety, she jumped over the tail and threw an energy ball at the spear, only to be beaten by another energy ball, glowing a brilliant red. Faye glanced up at the source and locked eyes with Tristan, whose anger matched hers.

"You all saw it!" Lord Godebeer cried, "The beast made a move on the King! I was only—"

Faye let out an angered cry as she shot a small

energy ball towards Lord Godebeer, only to have it ricochet off an agile guard's shield. "You know damn well that's a lie! He was making—"

"She tried to attack me! You saw it! Seize her!" Godebeer cried. The guards unsheathed their swords once more. Faye saw the King being carried out by a larger guard.

"Protect the King and Lord Godebeer!" one of the guards cried. Rinji let out an eerie hiss, bearing his teeth at the guards.

"*Idiots,*" Rinji hissed. "*Idiots with short tempers should never handle weapons.*"

Faye threw energy balls at a few guards; not large enough to do damage, but strong enough to stun them for a little while. "Rinji, protect the others, I'll—"

"*My bond is with you, little one. I am here to protect you!*" Faye was about to object when she felt an arrow whiz past her ear. She was about to attack the guard when she saw Zachariah running towards him. In one swift move, he threw a dagger at the guard's weapon. Seeing this, the guard began to attack with his fists. Zachariah ducked and dodged the brutal punches with ease and gave the guard a swift kick in the jaw.

"Faye, get out of here!" the huntsman yelled, failing to notice the five guards sneaking up from behind.

"Zachariah!" Faye called out, but it was too late. One guard had hit the back of the huntsman's head with the hilt of their sword, knocking him to the ground. She ran towards the gap and jumped, not knowing whether or not she would make it across. Suddenly, she felt something wrap around her waist and instead of landing, she continued to fly... away from the palace. She looked down at her waist and saw the green and yellow scales from Rinji's tail wrapped securely around her.

Everything happened in slow motion.

Faye watched as Zachariah was dragged into the palace. Princess Dara was being held by two guards; one was holding her arms, while the other desperately tried to restrain her kicking feet, and Tristan was surrounded by multiple guards, his hands glowing, but his eyes gazed up at her with a look of relief.

"Rinji! Stop! Take me back!" she cried out, gazing back down at the ground as things started becoming smaller.

"That is one thing I cannot do, little one," Rinji replied harshly. *"I told you, I am here to protect you."*

CHAPTER SEVENTEEN: THE FLOWERS

WHAT ARE YOU DOING?!" Faye held onto Rinji's tail for dear life as he continued to fly farther away from Arana.

"You need to clear your mind, and being there wasn't helping. Hold on, little one!" Rinji stayed afloat for a few moments.

The clouds seemed unreal, colored in a mixture of yellows and oranges thanks to the sun. Rinji continued to fly, Faye's short hair whipping around in the wind. Although the view was breathtaking, that did not stop Faye's frustration from growing.

"Rinji! Take me back! Just—just take me back! I'm done!" Faye yelled, feeling the impatience inside of herself growing.

"You want to go back!? FINE," Rinji's thoughts yelled

in her mind. *"Let's go back."* Rinji tucked his wings in slightly and dove through the clouds. Faye's anger was suddenly replaced with fear as she felt her heart jump to her throat. The wind whipped viciously around her as she saw a palace coming to view. She recognized the green and brown colored tapestries and realized she was back in Janulai.

"Wait...wait, Rinji! This isn't Arana!" she screamed as they swooped inches above the palace walls. Faye could hear the shouts from the guards as they whizzed over their heads.

"You wanted to go back...so I'm taking you back!" Rinji roared. *"This is what you are coming back to, little one."*

Faye saw the Hoof of Pig tavern as she flew overhead. "Watch out!" Faye cried to the villagers; some screamed and ducked for cover while others dove out of the way of the helpless girl being pulled by Rinji's tail. They continued to fly until a large field was within sight. Faye's heart sank as she recognized the field; the house was nowhere to be found, but the memory was still as fresh as the day the fire happened.

"You wanted to come back," Rinji snorted. *"Well, here you are."*

"This isn't what I meant, and you know it!" the young girl yelled, blinking back tears. "You and I share thoughts...memories...you should *know* what this place is!" Faye saw the expression in Rinji's eyes turn from irritated to regret. She turned her back to Rinji and began slowly walking up the hill; each step heavier than the last, until she made it to the top. She gazed down at the soil, where her hut once stood, and sat down. The tears rolled down her cheeks as she cried softly. "Mom….dad...I miss you," she whispered. "I-I should be with you," she gasped softly. After a few moments of silence, she turned her head to find Rinji already beside her, tears in his eyes as well.

"The morning of the fire," Faye cleared her throat, "my father and I...we went to the market to run a few errands. My father wanted to surprise my mother with a gift, because her birthday was the following day. He bought her this...this beautiful necklace," Faye smiled softly as she recalled the memory vividly, "it was very beautiful...a gold leaf holding a small red ruby; it was the prettiest thing I had ever seen. I wanted to buy my mother something too, but I had no money. My father told me, 'don't worry, darling...there are many ways of telling...and showing...someone you care for them. Why not make something special for her? I'm sure she'll love that."

"Faye, you—you don't—"

"So what do I do?!" Faye's bottom lip began to tremble at the memory. "I make myself promise to go to the forest after the marketplace and find some beautiful flowers for her, knowing she loved the small flowers that grew by the Grandfather Tree." Faye's fingers began to play with the long blades of grass that surrounded her. "When we got home, I was so tired from the walk that I fell asleep. By the time I woke up, it was night time.

"I—I panicked," Faye choked back her tears, "thinking —th-that my mother would be so upset if I didn't get her those—those stupid flowers. So what do I do? I sneak out of the house, and go to the forest to gather flowers...because I was so stubborn and certain that she would be utterly miserable without flowers. When I think about that night," Faye hesitated as she wiped more tears off her cheeks, "it felt...different...the air. At the time, I was so focused on getting the flowers, I didn't...*care*, I guess is the correct word? Well, by the time I picked enough flowers and left the forest...I saw the purple glow, and—" Faye sniffled as she grabbed her right arm and unrolled the sleeve, showing the burn marks. "I panicked when I saw the fire. It wasn't a normal fire...I knew it was magic. So, what do I do? I try to use my magic — magic that I was barely good at — to stop the fire...

211

"When that didn't work, I ran to the door and tried to open it." She recalled the sensation her arm felt that night; as if a hot, dull-pointed knife was digging into her skin and trying to go deeper...she heard her younger self scream in agony as she felt someone pull her away. "Marcus saved my life...but I wish he could've saved my parents." Faye glanced up at Rinji, tears still streaming down her cheeks. "I should have been in there with them! I should be dead..." She covered her face in her hands, wanting to hide herself from the world. She could feel Rinji's snout nuzzle her arm, and she embraced him in a hug. "They're right," she mumbled. "Listerah...Godebeer...Marcus...I can't do this. I'm just," Faye sighed softly, "little Faye; too young to understand the world, and too weak to show any true power."

"*Oh, little Sorceress,*" Rinji thought sadly. "*Have you not yet realized how wrong you are?*" He pulled away until their eyes locked. "*Yes, you are young...but you are also incredibly powerful. I don't think most people your age would find themselves this close to a dragon.*" Faye's mind flashed to the memory of when she first met Rinji. "*You are one of the bravest humans I have encountered in my lifetime, and believe me...I've been here for a long time. You are destined for great and wonderful things.*"

Faye's heart skipped a beat at the familiar words that echoed in her mind, recalling High Sorcerer Cato and her meeting with him eight years ago.

"He granted you the gift for a reason," Rinji assured the young girl. *"He saw something unique in you...why can't you see it, too?"*

"Because," Faye sighed, "I—"

"There is no reason or excuse, Faye; there's no possible reason for you being unable to see the talent you have inside you...take it from the creature you're able to communicate with."

"I just—I want to be—"

"—the best? You can't — not right away, at least," Rinji corrected himself. *"No one is born being the absolute best. 'We're born to do our best, and to do things that are for the best...for everyone.' Sound familiar?"* Rinji retorted, a sparkle in his eye. Faye smirked and fiddled with her robe as the familiar words echoed in her mind. *"Faye...your heart is the size of a dragon's; you have so much love and compassion for everyone, you want to make sure things are right. Can't you see?! You're alive, because you are destined to help make things right...to the best of your ability; and if all else fails, that's when you turn to your companions. No one can do something like this alone."*

Faye smiled at Rinji as she traced her fingers on the side of his face; his scales felt rough against her skin. *"I miss them, Rinji,"* she thought sadly.

"I know you do," Rinji's voice echoed in her mind, a feeling of calmness rushing through her body. *"They're never far from you, if you keep their memories in your heart."* Faye was about to say something, when her stomach began to growl softly. *"Come. Let's go to—"*

"Marcus' hut," Faye pleaded. *"I need to grab a few other things before we go back to Arana."*

"Faye, I—I don't think—"

"Please, Rinji? You don't have to worry about anyone seeing you; his hut is pretty isolated." she thought eagerly. She considered the extra ingredients left behind, and hoped—

"I don't think Marcus will be there, child," Rinji interrupted, reading her thoughts. *"However, if you truly want to go, then we need to hurry."*

***

"Wait outside, Rinji," Faye suggested. "I'm just gathering a few things, and then we can be on our way."

The hut felt cold and empty when Faye entered; small cobwebs occupied the corners, yet everything was still in its place. She traced her fingers alongside the edge of the chairs, remembering her classes she had with Marcus and how at the time she had wanted to be anywhere else but in that chair.

"I wish I could take it back," she thought sadly. She didn't hear a response from Rinji, and was thankful for the moment of silence. Sighing softly, she headed towards the cabinet and began to gather a few vials filled with different colors. She stored them in her satchel, and gave one last look around the hut, until her eyes locked on Marcus' closed door. Curiosity got to the best of her as she headed down the small corridor to his room. She placed her hand on the door-knob...

"Faye! We have company!" Rinji's voice warned her. Faye froze as she heard horses coming closer.

"Rinji, get out of here!" Faye yelled. *"It's the King's guardsmen!"* Sure enough, as she ran outside of the hut, she saw green and brown tapestries peek over the hill, followed by fifteen horses; each horse was occupied by a guardsman, fully dressed in protective armor. Rinji gave out a warning growl, causing the horses to skitter around, anxious to leave. Faye eyed the guardsmen, one of them looking very familiar.

"You," she pointed to the blond guardsmen with the large scar on his face. "I know you! You were one of the drunks at the—"

"The tavern?" he interrupted, his voice deep and scruffy. "Yeah, I remember you. You hid your Mark pretty well," he recalled. Faye's hands began to feel warm. She glanced down and saw her hands begin to glow a soft green. "I wouldn't do that if I were you," he warned. As she looked up, another guardsman doused the Sorceress with a bucketful of water. "There," he laughed, "now you can't shoot any more of them magic balls at me." Faye could feel Rinji's anger swell inside her; she had to fight the urge to scream, which proved to be difficult.

"Where does he get the...the audacity—?!" Rinji let out a loud growl, baring his teeth towards the guardsmen.

"Rinji, don't," Faye warned, *"guardsmen aren't the same as knights; they get away with a lot more than this...let's not give them any reason to get creative."* The anger inside her was stronger, much to Faye's dissatisfaction. "You never answered my question," Faye's voice was more determined, if not aggressive. "My friend here doesn't like strangers."

"The King demands to see you," the blond guardsmen announced. "We are here to escort you to the palace."

"He'll have to get through me first," Rinji growled loudly, still baring his teeth.

216

"Then tell the King that we—"

"I ain't a messenger boy, brat!" the guardsman spat. "I'm to get you to the castle, by any...means...necessary," he finished with a grin.

"That's not what *I* recall the King saying," a voice challenged. The other guardsmen looked behind them and suddenly made an opening. Faye sighed softly in relief when she saw High Sorcerer Ezra. He was dressed in a red silk shirt, dark pants, and an ivory cape tied loosely around his neck. His bluish-green eyes stared at the drenched Sorceress, then towards the blond guardsman. "I also don't recall King Leroi instructing you to douse the guest in water—freezing water, from the looks of it," he sighed impatiently as he saw Faye shiver. He undid his cape and walked over to the Faye, carefully eyeing Rinji, who began to growl softly.

"Rinji," Faye whispered, her eyes never leaving the guardsman.

"That's okay," Ezra assured, a dazzling smile on his face, "He knows to protect you from anyone; especially Bates," he nodded towards the blond guardsmen, who glanced at Faye, then looked towards his comrades. "Just trying to keep you warm," he announced as he wrapped the ivory cape around the young girl. "By the way," he whispered, a hint of amusement in his voice, "that was quite some entrance you and Rinji made."

"*Unintentional, he means,*" Faye thought to herself.

"*He doesn't have to know that,*" Rinji retorted, causing Faye to chuckle softly.

"So I see Kardos was right," Ezra glanced up at Rinji. "No spell?" he asked softly. Faye shook her head. "I knew there was something special about you!" he continued to whisper, his eyes lit with excitement and his smile growing in size. "Come!" Ezra said loudly, turning on his heel and heading towards his horse, "I must escort you to the palace."

"Wha—wait!" Faye called out. Ezra whirled around and raised an eyebrow. "Tristan...Zachariah...Princess Dara...they're still at Arana. They were dragged away—"

"Tristan can handle himself," Ezra said nonchalantly. He turned to Faye, who had a look of worry in her eyes. "Hmm...women," he muttered softly. "Alright, fine. We will get them out of their mess, just follow me. Oh, but Rinji..."

"He can fly just fine—"

"It's not that, Faye. There was an attempt made, a few nights ago...Jedrek's Shadowed Dragon Whisperers were spotted. It's for the safety of the King," he looked up at Rinji, then leaned in towards Faye. "He can understand me, right?" he whispered.

"Faye, it's alright." Rinji nodded slowly. *"I wouldn't want to cause harm to the King. Besides,"* Rinji glanced towards the forest, *"I need sustenance; those horses are rather tempting to me,"* he confessed. *"You know what to do if you need me; just call my name, little one."* He glanced at Ezra once more before expanding his wings and taking to the skies. Ezra and the guardsmen shielded their faces with their arms as a gust of wind blew viciously around them. *"Stay out of trouble, little one!"* Faye watched as her winged friend flew over the treetops, eventually disappearing from sight.

"Faye?" Ezra called once more. "I don't like to repeat myself, darling...and I personally wouldn't want to keep the King waiting, would you?"

CHAPTER EIGHTEEN: THE MYST

THE HALL SMELLED LIKE SMOKED MEAT. In fact, every hall Faye weaved through in King Leroi's palace had the same scent. Faye took another deep inhale and smiled at the pleasing aroma.

"It smells like King Leroi had a successful hunting trip," Ezra observed aloud before whispering softly, "that means he's in a good mood. Luck seems to be on our side, Faye." He led her through one more corridor until they stopped at a pair of large polished doors with the symbol of a large oak tree carved into it. Two servants opened the doors, and Faye gasped at the beauty of the dining hall. A large banquet table that occupied the room was set up with enough food to feed at least half of her village; some servants were quickly running around the room, lighting the torches that occupied the walls, while others were setting up musical instruments in the corner.

"Someone enjoys music," Faye raised an eyebrow to Ezra, only to be surprised as he handed her a plate of food.

"He must have had a *very* successful hunting trip," he remarked, sounding a little surprised. "By the way, I could hear your stomach growling since we entered the palace." Faye's cheeks quickly heated up as she looked away from Ezra and began eating some of the food on her plate; she couldn't believe the amount of flavor in the small portion of food. Suddenly, the doors opened and a tall, thin man with curly white hair dressed in an elegant green and brown tuxedo hurried to inspect the servant's work. He took notice of the table full of food and wine, adjusting the small glasses that balanced perfectly on his long, pointed nose.

"This will do better towards the center," he waved his fingers in front of the large plate of fruit. His voice was harmonious and airy, as if he were singing instead of speaking. He spun around, and even that simple movement looked like a dance until he stopped abruptly and stared at Faye and Ezra. "I'm sorry," he blinked a few times, "I don't remember *guests* being invited inside." His voice was still airy, yet this time a chill ran down Faye's spine as she slowly tried to hide the plate of food.

"It's alright, Whit," Ezra held a hand in the air casually. "She is here on special request: mine," he explained, a sudden twinkle in his eye.

Whit walked over to Faye, a finger to his chin as he eyed her outfit. "Well, at least she is wearing green," he sighed in defeat. "It'll have to do."

"Faye Haybear," Ezra sighed tiredly, though his smile was unwavered, "allow me to introduce King Leroi's majordomo, Whit Timrek. Whit, my...overly uptight friend," Ezra sighed once more before taking the plate of food covertly from behind Faye's back and giving her a quick wink. "This is Faye Haybear; Sorceress from our very lands of Janulai, here for an important meeting with the King."

"I wasn't informed of such meetings!" Whit exclaimed, taking the plate of food from Ezra's hands. "If she wants to meet the King, she'll have to wait, like the others!"

"But—"

"That's all I have to say on the matter! Besides," he

222

gave Faye a final, if not quick, glance. "What business does a *child* have in the palace?" Faye was about to say something, until Ezra placed a hand on her shoulder and she looked up at him. He shook his head subtly, raised an eyebrow, and smiled back at Whit.

"You're *absolutely* right, Whit! What *was* I thinking," he said loudly as he turned Faye by the shoulders and guided her towards the door. "Wait for it…" he whispered, then before exiting, stated loudly, "I shall leave it up to the King's majordomo to inform His Majesty that an *UnShadowed* Dragon Whisperer *had* to leave because she did *not* have a scheduled meeting."

A large crash was heard from behind them. Faye and Ezra whirled around to see Whit standing stiff, his face paler than his hair and the plate and small portion of food scattered around him.

"D-d-d-d-Dragon Whisperer?! Sh—she—?!" he squeaked in response.

"Yes, our own Faye of Janulai is one of the Dragon Whisperers; the youngest one, if I am not mistaken, and the *Varjo* have yet to find her, or her dragon—you know, the one that flew above the palace not too long ago? However, you are *absolutely* right; she needs an appointment. So, we'll just be on our way—"

"Just a moment!" Whit quickly ran towards Faye

and pulled her by his side. "Of—of *course* she has an appointment!" Whit exclaimed in nervous tittering, patting Faye on the head awkwardly. "Goodness, you must be starving, Ray!"

"Erm, it's Faye—"

"You there!" Whit pointed to a servant. "Get her some food and ale, and...WHO MADE THIS MESS?! Clean it up at once!" He pointed to the broken plate on the ground, turned back around and guided Faye to one of the seats. In an instant, she was provided with a larger portion of food and a full glass of ale. "I—I hope everything is to your liking, madam," Whit chuckled nervously. "I—I shall let King Leroi know you are here at once!" He spun towards the door and gracefully closed the doors behind him. The servants looked at each other, chuckling softly as a loud, high pitched shriek was heard down the hall.

"I love it when he gets like that," Ezra laughed. "Come along," the High Sorcerer snatched the plate once more from Faye, grabbing a bit of meat, "the King is waiting for us in the library."

Faye blinked in confusion. "Wh—wait, wasn't Whit..."

"All the means of a distraction," Ezra bowed before Faye with an amused spark in his eye. As he clapped his hands, the extravagant array of food from the banquet hall vanished, leaving the servants standing around, gawking at the once fully decorated room. The banquet hall suddenly turned to a smaller dining area, one Faye assumed was the servant's dining quarters.

"I hate when he does that," she heard one of the servants mutter. "That food looked delicious…"

"Don't worry, I will bring you some of those delectable meals tonight," Ezra promised the grumbling servants, "but until then, keep Whit away!" With that, he turned on his heel and walked off, grabbing Faye by the crook of her elbow.

"So, did King Leroi even *have* a hunting trip?" Faye asked, confused.

"No. This was planned earlier today; I just enjoy seeing Whit run around panicking."

Faye chuckled softly, not knowing who was worse: Ezra and Whit, or Godebeer and…

Before she could ask Ezra about Tristan, he stopped walking. "Let's see," he muttered, turning towards Faye and brushing some dirt off of her hooded cloak. "This cloak is rather unfitting," he stated as his hands glowed a brilliant yellow. "Too baggy. Let me just—"

"Please don't ruin it," Faye asked him, holding his hand down. "Marcus…he made this for me."

Ezra rubbed his index finger under his nose and sighed. "Well, he didn't know you were going to meet a King, did he?" he quipped as he touched a small piece of the green fabric with his fiery hand; yellow smoke soon covered the cloak, cleaning it and trimming it more to her size. "There," Ezra sighed contently, "you still have his fabric," he eyed her, hesitating for a moment, then he turned around and placed his hands on the doors, "and I understand why Marcus made your cloak the way he did. " Faye raised an eyebrow and looked down at her cloak.

"Ezra, change it back!" she hissed. The cloak, once baggy, now fit her perfectly, showing the curve of her body and accentuating her physical attributes a little more. Faye tried moving the hooded cloak around to make it loose around her chest, but to no avail. "Ezra!"

"You can thank me later," Ezra whispered quickly as they walked into the library.

Sitting in a large, green throne decorated with gold plated leaves was King Leroi. His jet black hair curled slightly and just touched his shoulders, and his crown was simple yet elegant; gold and bronze metals entwined together to make an elaborate headpiece. In one hand, he held a large bronze chalice, and the other held a small book. He looked up towards Ezra and Faye

226

with excitement in his emerald eyes. Faye looked down immediately as they both bowed before royalty.

"Your Majesty! Enjoying your book?" Ezra observed as he regained his posture. Faye felt herself being pulled up and made a mental note not to bow for a long time. *"I must have looked awful,"* she thought to herself as she blushed.

"Relax, little one. I'm sure the King is used to it," Rinji's voice assured her. Faye sighed softly in relief. Hearing Rinji's voice meant he wasn't too far from where she was, and she instantly relaxed.

"Eh, 'just words on paper', Whit says...HA!" the King shouted, "Books...now *there's* true magic! Where else can I have adventures like the ones in books?"

"Have you ever ridden a dragon?" Faye blurted out, only to blush even more.

"Now...that might have made you look foolish," Rinji's voice cautioned. *"Just a little bit."*

King Leroi stared at the Sorceress for a few moments, each silent breath longer than the first. Suddenly, he let out another laugh. "No! No, I haven't, Dragon Whisperer; but I'm sure you'll let me ride your dragon one day!"

Faye sighed in relief as she smiled. "It would be an honor, Sire."

"So, this is the Dragon Whisperer you spoke about," King Leroi observed aloud, staring at Faye as he rose from his seat. He snapped his fingers at a servant holding a pitcher. "She certainly doesn't *look* like a child," he commented as he watched the servant pour a purple liquid into his chalice.

"Not anymore," Ezra muttered under his breath, causing Faye to blush. He glanced at her and whispered, "still waiting for that 'thank you', by the way."

"Y-Your Majesty," Faye stepped forward, awkwardly curtsying once more, "my friends...they're still in Arana after a *misunderstanding* between Lord Godebeer and—"

The King let out a loud bark of a laugh. "Godebeer? That complacent blowhard?" he motioned towards two empty chairs as he went to sit back down in his green throne. "Hope Tristan gave him a proper thrashing."

Faye sat down and fiddled with her newly tailored robe. "The thing is, there's a Princess with him...and my friend, a huntsman of the Elven Clan," Faye saw the stern line the King's mouth made as she quickly looked away, "and—and with the Queen Regent's...opinion...on the Elven Clan—"

"I remember that battle," he muttered. "Cowards, the lot of them; but I'm sure this was before your friend's time." Faye looked back up at King Leroi, hope in her eyes.

"Yes, Your Highness! Please," she controlled the tremble in her voice, "please get them out. They meant no harm—not that any was caused, if Godebeer hadn't tried throwing that spear, and Rinji—"

"Rambling," Ezra warned in hushed tones. Just then, loud footsteps were heard down the hall, only growing louder.

"Your Majesty!" a familiar voice called just from outside the door that slowly opened. "Y-your Majesty," Whit called out of breath, "you have visitors—" Whit paused and stared at Faye and Ezra, a look of disbelief in his eyes. "Wha—but you—and she—the-the banquet—" Whit's eyes flashed with realization as to what occurred and shot an icy glare at the High Sorcerer.

"Whit!" Ezra greeted casually, "so nice of you to be here."

"Yes, yes, what do you want, Whit?! Can't you see I have company?" King Leroi grumbled, drinking more out of his chalice.

"Wh—well, yes, Sire! I-I was trying to—"

"Actually," the King interrupted nonchalantly, "it's good you're here. I need your assistance."

Whit's demeanor changed suddenly from out of

breath to calm and poised. "Anything, Sire!"

"I need you to take a few guardsmen and travel to Arana; our young Dragon Whisperer here has friends still with the Queen Regent."

The corner of Whit's lip began to twitch. "Arana?! B-b-but Sire! That will take *days* to get there!"

King Leroi raised an eyebrow at his majordomo. "Then I suggest you start going *now*," he suggested, his tone resolute.

Whit inhaled deeply, his chest puffing out as he glared subtly at Ezra, then exhaled quickly as he bowed. "Yes, Your Majesty." Giving one more glance towards Faye, he turned on his heel and hurried out the door.

"Dragon Whisperer," the King took another swig from his chalice, "I helped you. Now, you can help my Kingdom."

Faye blinked in confusion. "Erm, I—I don't—?"

"Over in Baroody, Jedrek and his...his...shadow army," his knuckles turned white as he clenched onto his chalice, "have been taking over lands one by one, already having Salzar in his possession." Faye's heart stopped as she glanced up at Ezra, who seemed to know what she was thinking.

"Kardos is alright, Faye," Ezra assured the frantic girl. "He's enroute to Janulai as we speak."

"We need your gift, girl." King Leroi interrupted. "We need you to help defeat Jedrek and his army."

Faye blinked a few times. "With all due respect, Your Majesty, I—I just want to find Marcus."

"You need to forget about him."

"I will do no such thing!"

"Do you want Janulai to have the same fate as Salzar?!" the King's tone sounded impatient as his face turned hard, "it is your *duty* to aid *your* Kingdom in time of need!"

She turned away from the King as she thought about her small village; Marcus, the Hoof of Pig Tavern, Little Verna...the Baker's family...

"They're all dead," she recalled the *Varjo* hiss in the baker's ear. Faye sighed as she turned to face the King.

"I am here to serve you," she decided, "but I am also going to look for—"

"Your hand," Ezra whispered. She looked at the High Sorcerer in confusion before he lifted her right hand. "I thought Kardos said the Mark was on your back."

"It...it was."

Faye stared in awe at her right hand; from her index finger and thumb down her arm was covered in shimmering scales. The scales were slowly covering what was left of her skin. "Ezra," she looked up in confusion, "why doesn't this hurt?! The one on my back burned; like I was on fire."

"I—I honestly do not know," he exhaled, brushing his finger along the scales. She saw his eyes glance just behind her as he shook his head softly. Faye turned around slightly, still being held onto by Ezra, and saw Kardos at the doorway. Kardos wore a simple blue hooded traveling cloak, covering most of his silk white blouse and brown pants, which was covered in specks of mud and dirt.

"Your Majesty," Kardos bowed towards the King. "Thank you for having me. Ezra," he nodded towards the other High Sorcerer, then his eyes locked onto the young Sorceress. "Faye, the Princess...is she—?"

"She's safe, Kardos." Faye replied, seeing the look of relief flash in his eyes. "She's with Zachariah in—"

"Kardos, are you seeing this?" Ezra asked him, lifting up Faye's hand, which was now completely covered in scales. Kardos stepped closer to examine Faye's hand. "It's nothing like I've ever seen," Ezra finished.

"We should ask Tristan—"

"We can't."

"Where is he?"

"Having a play date with Godebeer."

"Why am I not surprised?" Kardos sighed, pinching the bridge of his nose.

"What's happening?! I thought the Mark only stayed in one spot!" Faye pulled away from Ezra's grasp and backed away quickly, grabbing her scaly hand as if to protect it.

"Faye, please...calm down," Kardos' voice was soft yet authoritative.

"Don't tell *me* to calm down!" she hissed. "You don't even know what this is! The only person I think that might know, is the one person I'm trying to find that *you* told me to forget about; you *both* said that!" she glared at Kardos and the King, who suddenly looked terrified.

"Guards!" he barked. In an instant, four guards ran into the room and surrounded the King, blocking him from Faye's sight.

"Faye," Ezra's voice was cautious. She glanced at him and noticed his eyes went from her face to her hands. She looked down and gasped at the purple fire engulfing her hands.

"Get the King out of here," Kardos commanded. "*NOW!*" The guards quickly ushered the King outside of the room with Kardos only following to close the doors.

"Th-this," she raised her hands up slowly, "keeps happening. Why?" Faye shook her hands in desperation until the purple flames eventually died down.

"You mean this has happened before?" Kardos raised an eyebrow. "When, exactly? Be specific, Faye."

She glanced at the two High Sorcerers, each showing curiosity and concern. "Well, it usually happens when I get angry or upset; Marcus always told me I need to curb my emotions, but—what?" Faye saw the look of concern multiply in their eyes as they looked at each other.

"You think it will work?" Ezra asked. Kardos stared at Faye, sighing deeply.

"It has to."

Ezra gazed at Faye, tapping his bottom lip with his index finger quickly, then glancing over at one of the long couches. "Lay there," he commanded. Faye did as told and nervously played with her fingers. "Don't be nervous, Faye," Ezra calmly whispered. "I won't hurt you, I've done this many times. I'm going to put you in a trance. Think of it as...seeing things as another person." He moved his hands around until a white substance floated around his hands. "This is Myst, Faye. Have you heard of it?" The young girl shook her head. "This will make you sleep, and will help us see everything in your mind. Things," he sighed, "sometimes forgotten, or blocked, where they can't be remembered. It allows us to see your memory from all angles."

"Does it hurt?" Faye asked.

Ezra pouted, his brows furrowing at the question. "Actually no," he sighed, "I never feel anything," he winked playfully at Faye. "You're going to probably get dizzy and lightheaded after this, hence why I am having you lay still. Now, you have to tell Rinji not to interfere. That is *very* important."

Faye nodded. *"Rinji, I don't know if you can—"*

"I can always hear you, little one," Rinji's voice assured her.

"Ezra is going to use some kind of myst on me." Faye took a nervous breath as she saw Ezra fiddling with the myst between his fingertips. *"He said you can't interfere, so it's safe to assume my emotions are going to go into overdrive."* There was silence.

"Be careful, Faye."

Faye smiled at Rinji's concern, then nodded to Ezra. "I'm ready." The Myst began to flow from Ezra's steady hands to Faye's head, circling around her face slowly as she inhaled the sweet smell of lavender. "Not your...n-normal..."

"I changed it a little. Folks seem to like lavender,"

Ezra smiled softly. "Now, close your eyes, and count backwards from ten."

"Teehhn…."

***

Faye opened her eyes once more, only to find herself standing in the middle of the woods of Janulai. Standing right beside her were Kardos and Ezra, who looked just as curious as she did.

"Home sweet home," Ezra announced, though it didn't feel like home. She looked behind her and saw the Grandfather Tree, once a mighty strong tree now decayed and rotted. Leaves were losing their green color, as was much of the rest of the foliage in the woods. "Something's off," Ezra muttered. "Has this ever looked so…dreary?" he asked Faye.

The young girl shook her head. "Not that I can remember," she confessed. Kardos' body tensed as he gripped his glowing sword and slowly turned his head to the left.

"We're not alone in this Myst," he growled. "Show yourself," he commanded. His voice was unwavering and firm as it echoed through the wooded area. After a few moments of tense silence, a figure appeared from the shrubbery. He stood tall with his hood concealing his face, though his amethyst eyes gave him away.

"What are the *Varjo* doing here?" Faye asked. The *Varjo* raised his hands in surrender. Faye noticed his hands were shaking.

"Please," he called out, his voice distorted but somewhat familiar to the young girl, "I-I mean no harm, I assure you. I need to show you something," he pointed to an opening. "It will explain much." His amethyst eyes focused on Faye, and the young girl couldn't shake the feeling of familiarity gnawing at her mind. "Please, Dragon Whisperer."

Faye glanced up at Ezra, his hands still glowing softly as he let out an annoyed groan.

"Fine," Ezra huffed, "but if there is a hint of a trap anywhere...I will gut you." Ezra's voice was in hushed tones, yet still intimidating. The *Varjo* motioned for the three to follow him as he walked out into the opening. In the field there was a young couple running around and playing. The man was chasing after a woman who was giggling playfully. He eventually grabbed her by the waist and pulled her down, both of them laughing and out of breath. "How romantic," Ezra mumbled, clearly unmoved by the couple. "What does this have to do with Faye?" he challenged.

The *Varjo* eyed Faye as he pointed to the male. "Look closer. Doesn't he look familiar?" In that moment, they were suddenly closer to the couple. Faye looked at Ezra uncomfortably. "They can't see you," the *Varjo* assured her. Faye glanced at the *Varjo* and nodded silently.

Faye gazed at the man, and couldn't believe her eyes. She recognized the man's red hair, the freckles on his cheeks, the green eyes that would lovingly gaze at her when she was younger. "That's...that's my father, but I don't know the woman," she confessed. "That's not my mother." Unlike her mother, who had brown hair, this woman had long, blonde hair and gray eyes. Her skin was perfect, like it was made of porcelain. her fingers were long and slender as they played with her father's hair, sending a chill down Faye's spine.

"Oh, Viktor," the woman sighed. "This is all I've ever wanted. To be happy, free, and with the man I love." Faye's heart ached when she heard this stranger say those things to her father. "With our magic, we don't have to live in the world our parents created. We could create our own world," the woman nuzzled his chest, her eyes closed.

"Magic? My father didn't have—" Faye's words froze as Viktor twirled his fingers in the air and made a beautiful green rose out of the blades of grass and handed it to the woman. "Wait...he told me he didn't," she muttered to herself.

"I love you, Viktor," the stranger sighed, "and I always will." With that, she pulled him into a deep kiss. Just then, the Myst surrounded the four, leaving the happy couple behind.

"What's going on?" Faye asked, looking around at the sudden Myst.

"There's more to see," the *Varjo* explained. "Trust in me, both of you," he insisted as he looked at Kardos, who was glaring at the shadow demon. When the Myst finally cleared, they were at the top of a hill with Viktor once more, only he appeared a little older, more refined. There was a woman with him, someone Faye recognized instantly. Her brown hair that always curled at the bottom, and her smile that seemed to brighten the day.

"*That's* my mother," Faye stated with pride.

"Good job, Viktor," Ezra commented, nodding in approval. Faye was going to say something, but Viktor began clearing his throat.

"Sidara," his voice shook with nervousness, "You are the greatest thing to happen in my life. I only wish I had found you sooner...my life didn't start until I met you two years ago today..." he hesitated, and Sidara could tell.

"But...?"

Viktor sighed, "I haven't been honest with you." he confessed. Faye blinked in confusion. What did he lie to her mother about? "I...have the Gift of magic," he confessed. "I should have told you when I first met you. I'm so sorry, and if you want to—" Sidara laughed, shaking her head.

"Is that all?" she asked, her laughter ringing in the skies. Viktor looked at his significant other, a blank look on his face.

"'Is that all?' Well, I don't see what's so funny—" Sidara stopped Viktor from talking as she waved her hand in the air, her fingers dancing as flower petals circulated in the air until they made a bird. Viktor gaped in awe at the reveal of Sidara's Gift.

"They *both* had magic?" Kardos gasped.

"Lucky kid," Ezra added. "Most gifted children are lucky to have at least one member of their family with the Gift of magic, but two?"

Faye stood there, speechless. "They told me they didn't have magic. It was just—just on my mother's side," she stumbled through her words, staring at her parents in shock. "It...it skipped a generation..."

"No wonder we are perfect together!" Viktor

exclaimed happily. With that, he grabbed Sidara, pushing her down to the grass. As Sidara fell, the petals broke apart, falling to the ground once more.

Faye smiled at the love her parents had, but it did not last. A clap of thunder was heard over them, and when they looked up, purple and gray smoke filled the area until a woman with long black hair stood beside them.

"Well," she scoffed, "isn't this precious." Her eyes were a menacing gray as she glowered at the happy couple.

Viktor moved in front of Sidara in order to protect her. "Milla, please…"

A sharp intake of breath was heard from Ezra. Faye glanced up and saw the look in his eyes; it was one of shock and realization. "So that explains it," he murmured. "That explains so much."

CHAPTER NINETEEN: THE FIRE

MILLA, PLEASE CALM DOWN." Milla gazed down at her old lover, tears stinging her eyes. "SILENCE!" she yelled, a clap of thunder ringing over them. "This is what you leave me for?!" Milla pointed a slender finger towards Sidara. "For this little thing?!"

Viktor said nothing. He could only stare at the purple and black smoke that surrounded her, lifting her off the ground. "Milla, what's happened to you?" he asked. "You're not well. You've...changed."

Milla cackled loudly, tossing her head back. "Oh, Viktor. I've never felt better," Milla winked at her past love. "I unlocked a new power within me. A new world, like I've always wanted—like we always talked about," she cooed, "so I offer you this one last chance. Return to me, and have life eternal. Think about it, Viktor!" As she moved her hand in the air, black and purple smoke circled around him, lifting him to her level. "Eternal life! All the power in the world, all the realms under your command! Under *our* command," she whispered, giving him a kiss on the lips.

"That's enough, Milla," Sidara yelled. "He told you before, he doesn't want to be with you!"

"Silence!" Milla yelled, sending a blast of purple energy in Sidara's direction, knocking her to the ground.

Faye looked at Sidara in terror. "Mother!" she called out, forgetting she was inaudible to them. She glanced over at her father, the same horrified face matching her own. That look morphed from terror to rage as Viktor glared at Milla.

"Milla," he seethed, "I will never be with you. I don't care if you offer everlasting life, all the money or power in the world! That will never come close to the love I carry for Sidara. As a matter of fact," he stared into her gray eyes, his emerald green eyes lit with fury. "Tomorrow, I plan to go to High Sorcerer Cato to revoke my Gift of magic. I never wanted it in the first place."

Faye could see the tears in Milla's eyes as she dropped him to the ground. "You—you wouldn't!" she cried. "You would give up all that for *her!?*"

"I'd give up more, if I could," he replied, his face emotionless. "I never want to see you again, Milla. You hurt the one I love, so I shall make you suffer...by placing the banishment spell on you." Milla's face turned from saddened to fearful. "You are never to come near me or my family ever again." A brilliant green orb began growing around Viktor, growing in size. Once it hit Milla, it began pushing her away. "This spell will last for all eternity, and anyone sharing my bloodline is safe until they die...or you do." With that, he punched the ground, causing a large green flash to emit from the orb, forcing Milla to fly away. In the distance, Faye could see Milla disappear into a purple and black mass.

"Viktor?" Sidara called, standing up slowly. Viktor hurried over to her.

"Sidara! The baby...is it—"

"The baby is fine. I don't feel anything wrong. She's strong," Sidara commented, placing a hand on her stomach.

"Here we go," Ezra smirked. "That's you in there." Faye suddenly felt very awkward as she watched her parents each place a hand on Sidara's stomach. She glanced up at Kardos, who had a solemn expression on his face; his brows furrowed as he scanned the scene in front of them.

"How do you know it's a girl?" Viktor sighed. "It could be a boy."

Before Faye could hear Sidara's comment, the Myst took over once more. The scenery changed dramatically; from being in the fields on top a hill, they quickly made it in front of a hut as the sun began to set. Faye hesitated when she recognized the hut.

"No, no this can't be now..." Faye muttered to herself. She looked around until she spotted Milla. She stood by the edge of the woods, her dark hair flowing as if there was wind.

"This is my time now," the *Varjo* commented, "when I apologize for everything."

Faye raised an eyebrow. "I—I don't—"

The *Varjo* placed a hand on her shoulder. "You will, Faye. And you'll understand what I tried telling you in the first place."

Faye was more confused than ever. "Wait, *Varjo*—"

He sighed, shaking his head. "My name...is *Jaako*." With that, he disappeared in a puff of black and purple smoke. Faye blinked at the empty space.

"Jaako...that's what the *Varjo*—"

"Faye," Ezra interrupted. They both gazed at the *Varjo* that was now standing next to Milla.

"I can't go near them," she scoffed, "but *you* can. You know what you have to do." She had a malicious grin on her face as she pointed to the hut. The *Varjo* nodded and walked slowly to the hut, his hands lit with purple and black fire.

"Faye," Ezra whispered, "I don't—"

Before he could say anything, before Faye could even have a chance to turn away, the *Varjo* blasted multiple fireballs at the unknowing hut, causing it to explode into a giant mass of purple and black fire. Tears poured down Faye's cheeks as she cried softly as she witnessed the inescapable death of her parents.

Faye turned to the spot where Milla stood, a wicked smile on her face as she disappeared into the night.

"Oh, no." Ezra's voice sounded cracked. Faye followed his gaze with watery eyes. About twenty feet away stood a younger form of herself, coming from behind the *Varjo*.

"Mommy! Daddy!" the young girl cried as she ran to the burning house, trying to open the door, only to cry out in pain. The *Varjo* desperately grabbed onto her, despite her squirming. His hood fell backwards and revealed a face made of smoke. Faye watched as the younger version of herself stared in curiosity, reaching her hand towards his face. The *Varjo's* hand glowed a light purple and touched the top of the young girl's head. She became motionless, her curious hand dropping to the ground. Just then, a cloud of black smoke surrounded the two.

"What's going on?" Faye asked Kardos, who only remained silent. When the smoke evaporated, Faye spotted a familiar face, his caramel eyes scanning the area. He turned back to look for his master, only to find her gone.

Ezra placed a reassuring hand on Faye's shoulder as her eyes glared furiously at the sight of the man that she risked her life to find, only to discover he was only sent to destroy hers.

"Why?" Marcus cried aloud, his voice echoing in the night sky. "WHY!?"

***

Faye gasped for air, the lavender scent gone, as was the horrid scene that she witnessed. She looked up and saw Kardos' concerned blue eyes staring down at her.

Faye couldn't stop the tears from running down her cheeks. She got up too fast, causing the room to spin underneath her feet. She felt someone catch her, but didn't look to see who it was. "The fire," she gasped, re-imagining the purple and black flames destroying everything they touched. "It was intentional. Milla did it, but then again, she didn't." Faye put the pieces together as she looked from Kardos to Ezra, who glanced uneasily at each other.

"I knew something wasn't right," Kardos whispered to Ezra. "Faye, this explains the purple fire. When she struck your mother, it...it must have entered her body somehow. Part of Milla's power transferred to you...*that's* why the *Varjo* couldn't figure out who... *what*... you are."

"Until now," Ezra stared at Faye's scaly hand. "What Mar—*Jaako*—showed us might have given Milla the chance to—"

"She loved my father," Faye cried, "and because of that, they're dead...it was M-Marcus. He's a *Varjo*. He killed my parents. I don't think she even knew I existed, let alone survived." Suddenly, a clap of thunder was heard outside. The three looked out the large window and saw the black and purple clouds forming in the East. As lightning flashed, a piercing shriek filled the skies.

Ezra looked around nervously, and said what was burning in the back of Faye's mind. "Well, she knows who you are now...and she won't rest until you're dead."

To Be Continued

Acknowledgements

Wow...we did it! After more than two years of editing, plot bunnies (or DRAGONS, in this case) and patience, this is finally a book you can hold in your hands! It wouldn't have been possible without a few amazing people that I would like to recognize:

Jason Zucker, the very talented artist I was blessed to meet, took the time to listen to my ramblings of how I wanted the map to look...and I think he captured it perfectly. Find him on Facebook at **Jason Zucker**.

Ravenborn Covers did a fantastic job with the cover art! She took the time to ask me my vision of the cover (front and back), and went above and beyond my expectations. You can see more of her work on Facebook at **Ravenborn**.

About the Author

J.S. Castillo resides in East Taunton, MA with her husband and family. *The Mark of the Dragon Whisperer* is J.S. Castillo's first published work. Having a passion for writing, she can be found partaking in NaNoWriMo during the spring and winter.

Made in the USA
Middletown, DE
04 May 2017